SWEET TEA & BABY MAKES THREE

RACHEL HANNA

To my wonderful, loyal readers:
Thank you for loving the Sweet Tea B&B series. Although
this is the final book in the series, these characters will
always live in my heart. I hope they'll live in yours, too.
Thank you for reading my books. You'll never know how
much it means to me.

CHAPTER 1

KATE STOOD IN THE SMALL ROOM, HER HANDS sweating. It was one of those anxiety things that a person couldn't stop from happening. For her, it was a fluttering heartbeat and sweaty palms. Thank goodness she had a serious boyfriend because neither of those things would look good on a dating app.

"Hey, Kate?"

She turned to see a woman she'd met briefly a few minutes before standing in the doorway. "Yes?"

"You go on in about twelve minutes. We'll come get you shortly." She shut the door, and Kate could hear her jogging back down the hallway.

Everything moved so quickly in TV news, it seemed. She'd only briefly walked through the area where the set was, and she'd seen just a quick peek of the control room as they ushered her back to the small green room.

Traveling to Atlanta by herself to be on "Good Morning, Georgia" was a challenge. She was used to having Mia, her daughter, or Cooper with her most of the time. It had been a good while since she'd had to do anything major on her own. The two-hour drive to the city hadn't been so bad, minus the rush-hour traffic. She'd arrived just an hour ago, giving herself enough time to stop for coffee and a doughnut.

When the show had called to invite her to come talk about the honey business, she'd been surprised but grateful. Sales were down a bit, and she was determined to make the business profitable. Her daughter would go off to college in a little over a year, and she wanted to pay for that without Evie needing a bunch of loans.

"We're ready for you," the woman said. Kate was terrible with names, so she just smiled and nodded. "Right this way." The woman led her down the hallway toward the set area.

"Do you know how long my segment will be?"

"Probably about six minutes total. Three before commercial and three after. But don't quote me on that," she said, smiling at her.

Could she talk for six whole minutes about honey?

"Next up, we're going to chat with the owner of Sweet Charlene's, an innovative flavored honey company from our beautiful north Georgia mountains. Stay tuned!" The host, Muriel Nevins, was an Atlanta staple. She'd greeted Atlanta area citizens every morning for over twenty-two years.

"Okay, come on," the woman, who Kate now remembered was named Izzy, said as she led her to a plush blue chair across from Muriel. Kate was expecting Muriel to smile, shake her hand, and welcome her to the show. Instead, she got her makeup touched up and took a long sip of her coffee drink. She looked completely disinterested in having Kate there.

Kate sat and waited for instructions, feeling very out of place. She was more of a small-town woman now. All this technology and rushing around was making her feel more anxious. Hopefully, Muriel would make her feel more comfortable once they started chatting.

"It's so nice to meet you in per..." Kate started to say.

"Lita? She needs touching up. There's a shine on her forehead that's blinding me!" Muriel yelled. A makeup woman frantically ran toward Kate, a giant makeup brush in her hand. She moved it around Kate's face and then disappeared into the darkness.

"Five... four... three..." a man said from the shadows. Kate couldn't keep up with the pace of what was happening.

Suddenly, Muriel's face changed, a big smile replacing her frown from seconds before. It was amazing how quickly she could change. "Welcome back! My next guest runs a sticky but sweet business in the quaint North Georgia mountains. Sweet Charlene's honey is based on her late mother, and they have some new flavors this season. Please help me welcome Kate to our show." She turned, her pearly white smile on full display.

"Thanks for having me," Kate said, feeling like the new kid at school, standing in front of the classroom.

"So, tell me, what's different about your honey?"

"Well, we harvest all of it ourselves, and then we work with a local co-packer to add special flavorings. It's a family-owned business that we named in honor of our late mother, Charlene."

"Oh, that's lovely," Muriel said in her fakest voice. "How did you decide to become a beekeeper?"

"I… well, I'm not really a beekeeper. We have a guy who…"

"Uh huh. And what flavors do you have coming out?"

"Going into summer, we have a wonderful peach honey as well as a maple syrup infused honey."

"Sounds yummy," Muriel said, grinning as she

looked into the camera. "Where can our viewers find your honey?"

"Well, we have a website, but we're also at a lot of the local mountain festivals. You can also purchase it at our bed-and-breakfast, Sweet Tea B&B."

"Wonderful! I'm sure my staff will put your website link on our website. Isn't technology great?" she said, again smiling into the camera and not looking at Kate.

Realizing she was losing her small amount of airtime, Kate decided to be bold. "I'd also like to say that our honey is ethically harvested, and all of our flavors are natural and organic. We use no preservatives or chemicals in our honey, so it's safe for every person, regardless of age or health status."

Muriel glared at her. "That's nice to hear. Next up…"

"Oh, and honey has so many wonderful health properties. It's an anti-inflammatory, antioxidant, and an anti-bacterial. Ours also has the added benefit of tasting great!"

"Well, thanks for all of that great info, Kate! I'm afraid we've run out of time, though," she said, poking out her bottom lip. She turned toward the camera again. "Join us after the commercial break when I'll be with Chef Todd, cooking up a beautiful apple pie!"

"And we're out," the guy in the shadows said. Muriel's face dropped back to her normal scowl.

"Thanks so much for having me…" Kate said, reaching her hand out. Muriel looked at it.

"I don't shake hands. It's gross."

"Oh, sorry." Kate stood up, eager to get back to the green room and then out of the building.

"For future reference, if you should ever get a chance to be interviewed on TV again, it's common courtesy to allow the host to lead the conversation."

Kate nodded and started to walk away, but her sassy side got the best of her. "For your future reference, it's common courtesy to care about what your interviewee has to say and not just about smiling at the camera with your big, fake, way-too-white teeth."

She turned and walked out, leaving Muriel standing there with her mouth hanging open.

Mia held the fitted sheet in her hands and flung herself across the bed a little too far. She laid face first on the mattress, her nose smashed into the soft fabric.

She felt like a cow. Instead of saying hello to people, maybe she'd just moo from now on.

Pregnancy had been a learning experience, to say

the least. Parts of her body she never thought could get bigger had, in fact, gotten bigger. This included her nose spreading so wide that she was sure it would soon touch both her ears. Why in the world was her nose widening?

And then there was the lack of sleep because of the constant bathroom trips. Sure, there was a giant baby sitting on her bladder. It felt like the kid was occasionally doing tap dance routines on it. But she'd assumed the lack of sleep part came after the baby was born. Maybe this was just practice for years of sleepless nights in her future.

She was thrilled to be having a baby. After all, it was her dream. She was so grateful that God was blessing her with a new little life. This was everything she'd ever wanted. Her only wish was that her mother could be there, but that wasn't possible.

She turned onto her back and pondered how she was going to get up from this awkward position. With only a few weeks left of her pregnancy, Mia couldn't wait to get her body back. She would breastfeed, of course, but she'd have her internal organs back in their rightful homes. Lately, it felt like her stomach lived in her chest and her kidneys lived near her tailbone.

Mia sighed as she stared up at the moving ceiling fan. She couldn't be in a room without the ceiling fan running on high. Normally cold-natured, pregnancy had caused her to be constantly hot, like her baby was an internal furnace.

She and Travis had opted not to find out the sex of their baby, wanting to be surprised during the delivery. The nursery would be gender neutral, with lots of pale yellow, tan, and green. She hadn't gotten to work on it yet, but it was on the list of things to do as soon as the B&B slowed down for a few days. They had names picked out for either gender, and they were fine whether they had a boy or a girl. It didn't matter at all to either of them.

"Aunt Mia? Are you okay?"

She craned her head to see Evie standing in the doorway, a confused look on her face. "Oh, thank God, Evie! Can you help me up?"

Evie rushed over and pulled on her arms, carefully helping her sit up. "What happened?"

"I was trying to make the bed and sort of toppled over."

Evie giggled. "You looked like one of those stranded whales."

"You mean a beached whale? Thanks a lot!" Mia said, slapping Evie on her leg. "I thought you were at work?"

Evie had recently taken a part-time job at the local ice cream shop to earn money for college. She had one more year of high school, and then she'd be gone. Mia couldn't believe it.

"I was. My shift ended at noon. Is Mom back from Atlanta yet?"

"No. I expect her soon, though. She probably stopped for lunch." Evie looked uneasy. "What's going on?"

"What do you mean?"

Mia smiled. "Honey, you have a terrible poker face. I can see that something is bothering you."

She sighed and hung her head. "I need to talk to Mom about something, and she will not like it."

"Do you want to tell me what it is?"

She nodded. "My guidance counselor pulled me out of class yesterday and told me I could graduate early."

"How early?" Mia asked, her eyebrows knitted together.

"In three weeks."

"What?" Mia yelped.

"Apparently, my exam grades qualified me, and they can make it happen. I started applying to colleges last night."

"So you're going to do it?"

"I mean, why would I stay in school another year when I don't have to?"

Mia could understand her thinking. Who wanted an extra year of high school?

"And you're worried your mother is going to freak out?"

"You and I both know she will."

"She'll be so proud of you, Evie."

"I know, but she's not ready."

Mia smiled. "Are you ready?"

She shrugged her shoulders. "I think so. I'm going to hate leaving you and mom here, but I'm kind of excited about college." She laughed. "Never thought I'd hear myself say that."

"Where have you applied?"

"I've applied at a couple of schools in Atlanta, but my dream school is UGA." Many kids in the area wanted to go to The University of Georgia, but it was a tough application process. Few people got in, and Mia hoped Evie wasn't setting herself up for disappointment.

"I'm so proud of you, Evie," she said, reaching over and patting her knee. "When you first came here, it was hard on you. I know the transition was so difficult."

She giggled. "Yes, coming from Rhode Island to a southern mountain town was a little... challenging. But finding out I had an aunt, and a grandfather, was the best thing that's ever happened to me."

"So far," Mia said, putting her arm around Evie and pulling her close. "You've got such a big, bright future ahead of you."

"Thanks, Aunt Mia. Please don't tell my mom yet. I just need to figure out a way to tell her."

"You have to do it soon, okay?"

Evie nodded. "I know." She stood up and held out both of her hands. "Now, come on. I'll make the bed. I don't want you stranded here all day."

Cooper stood in front of the newest zip line and looked at Travis. "You think people will do this one?"

Travis laughed. "Only our most adventurous guests. That thing scares me!"

The new line was a lot longer than their others, and it went over a pretty deep valley, providing outstanding views if the person zipping through the air was willing to look down.

"Remember that one guy who was the adrenaline junkie? With the church group?"

"Oh, yeah! I think his name was Phil. He didn't act like a Phil. He acted like a..."

"Hawk?"

"I guess that would be a good name for a guy who likes to fly through the air."

Cooper sighed. "We're about to get so busy."

Travis sat on the picnic table. "Yeah. Now that winter is behind us and spring has officially sprung, this place is going to be hopping. This will be the first time I have to juggle a business and a baby."

"I don't think you're supposed to juggle babies, dude. Should I call the authorities?"

"You're a regular comedian."

He slapped Travis's shoulder. "You know I'll pick up the slack here as much as I can. That baby will be my niece or nephew."

Travis looked at him. "How do you figure that? You haven't even proposed to Kate yet."

"It's all in the timing, my friend."

"And what kind of timing are you looking for, Cooper? Do all the planets have to align for you to put a ring on that woman's finger?"

Cooper sat on the other side of the picnic table. "You know I've had a checkered past with women, Travis. A failed marriage. A failed engagement."

"What does that have to do with Kate?"

"What do you mean?"

"Do you love her?"

He stared at Travis. "Of course I do."

"Do you want to spend the rest of your life with her?"

"Absolutely."

"Then why the hesitation?"

"I guess I don't trust myself not to screw it up."

Travis laughed. "I'm sure you'll screw something up. That's the Cooper way."

"Not funny."

"Kate loves you, and you love her. Isn't that enough?"

"No. Lots of people love each other and end up divorced."

"You definitely shouldn't get a job writing greeting cards, man."

Cooper stood up and stretched his back. "I'll know when the time is right."

Travis joined him in standing. "I sure hope Kate is on the same timeline as you. She will not wait around forever, and she shouldn't."

As Cooper watched Travis walk toward his truck, he felt his guts clench. What was his problem? He loved Kate more than anything, and he wanted to call her his wife. Why was he having such trouble asking her to marry him?

Kate laid on the sofa, staring up at the ceiling fan. Somehow she'd managed to sneak into the B&B, grab a pint of butter pecan ice cream, and flop onto the couch without anyone noticing. Of course, Evie was still at school, and the guys were at the adventure center. She assumed Mia had gone out to run errands or something.

She watched as the blades of the fan went round

and round. There was something oddly mesmerizing about it. It felt like a meditation. Or maybe she was just giving herself severe vertigo. She didn't care. Any distraction from her embarrassing performance on Good Morning, Georgia was a welcome one.

The ice cream sat on her stomach, rising up and down as she breathed. She jammed the silver tablespoon into it once more, shoving the cold, sugar-laden treat into her mouth and moaning. There was just something about drowning one's sorrows in junk food. Broccoli could never do this for her.

"Dear Lord, this is the saddest thing I think I've ever seen."

She turned her head to see her very pregnant sister standing behind the sofa, her hands on her hips. "Don't judge me. You weren't there."

Mia walked over and sat on the other end of the sofa, pushing Kate's feet out of the way. "That bad?"

"Muriel Nevins is a horrible woman. Don't let her fake smile fool you. She's the devil." She scooped another giant bite and pulled it toward her face. Mia reached over and snatched the tablespoon from her hand, eating the bite herself.

"Ice cream will not solve this, Kate." She took the container of ice cream and set it on the coffee table.

"But shouldn't I at least try?"

Mia giggled. "No. Now, sit up and tell me what happened."

Kate groaned and sat up, her back against the arm of the sofa. "There's not much to say, really. Muriel wasn't interested in talking to me about Sweet Charlene's. She barely gave me any time at all. She talked over me, wouldn't let me say anything. I don't know why she has such a grudge against honey."

"Yikes. It sounds like Muriel needs to retire."

"Well, she certainly needs to go somewhere. I wanted to suggest somewhere really hot."

Mia slapped her leg. "Kate!"

She laughed. "Sorry, sis. How are you feeling today?"

"Fat, bloated, and nearing explosion status," Mia said, rubbing her ample belly.

"It won't be long now. I remember how miserable I felt with Evie those last few weeks."

"Yeah, but you're tall with a lot more room. I feel like a family of squirmy squirrels is living in my small body."

Kate chuckled. "I guess that's one way to describe it."

The phone rang across the room, startling Kate. She walked over and picked it up, ready to take a reservation for the B&B. Busy season was definitely coming quickly.

"Sweet Tea B&B, how can I help you?"

"Is this Kate?"

"Yes, it is."

"My name is Talia Simon, and I'm with Deacon's."

Deacon's was the largest grocery store chain in the southeast. Kate had no idea why this woman was calling her.

"What can I do for you?"

"I happened to be home this morning and saw your segment on Good Morning, Georgia."

Kate wanted to crawl under a rock with her ice cream. "Oh?"

"First, I could tell that Muriel lady didn't want to talk about your honey for some reason. Very odd. Anyway, I was very impressed by how you got the information out there, anyway. Nicely done."

"Thank you."

"We at Deacon's would like to meet with you about carrying your honey in our stores. We have over four-hundred locations, so it would take some changes on your end as far as manufacturing goes. We can help with those logistics."

Kate felt like she couldn't speak. Her tongue seemed to be cemented to the roof of her mouth. "I... um..."

"What is it?" Mia whispered, waddling closer to her.

Kate put her index finger to her lips. "I'm very honored you're so interested in Sweet Charlene's..."

"I know this is a lot to take in, so I'd like to come

meet with you if you don't mind? See the B&B and honey operation?"

"Of course," Kate stammered. "When would you like to come?"

"Next week if you have an opening?"

Kate quickly opened the reservation book and scanned the names. "We actually have an opening starting on Tuesday."

"Wonderful! I'll drive down from our Nashville headquarters on Tuesday."

"Great. I look forward to meeting you."

As she pressed end on the call, Kate stared at the phone in her hand.

"Who was that?"

"One of the heads of Deacon's."

"The grocery store?"

"Yes. They want to carry our honey in all of their stores."

Mia's eyes widened. "What? How many stores is that?"

"Over four hundred!" Kate said, a little too loudly.

Mia put her hand over her mouth. "Four hundred? How on earth would we do that?"

"I have no idea," Kate said. "But we'd better figure it out before Tuesday."

CHAPTER 2

EVIE SAT UP IN HER TREEHOUSE, STARING OUT OVER the mountains she'd come to love so much. She was almost an adult, but she would never stop loving the treehouse. It had been her saving grace when she moved to Carter's Hollow.

Today, she was thinking about her mother and how she was going to react when she found out Evie was graduating early. It wasn't the graduation part that was an issue; it was the leaving home part. She knew her mother would not be happy about it. She and Evie were so close, and they'd always only had each other. How could she leave her mom behind?

Leaving Sweet Tea B&B and her Aunt Mia would be almost as hard. Evie had wanted a real family her whole life, and now she had one. Part of her thought maybe she should just stay in school another year or graduate but delay college. Take one of those "gap" years.

A part of her wanted to stay close to home and get to know her new baby cousin that was coming soon, but she knew that wasn't logical. She needed to get on with her adult life after she graduated, or she might just end up like so many people who never make it to college.

"Got room for one more?" She looked down and saw Cooper standing at the bottom of the tree, smiling up at her.

"Always." She loved Cooper every bit as much as she loved her own father. She didn't want to admit out loud that she might've loved Cooper even more. Even though her relationship with her dad was better, it was still complicated at times. On the other hand, Cooper had been there for her from day one, and she knew she could count on him.

He climbed to the top and slid next to her. "That gets harder every time," he said, breathless. "Maybe we need to install one of those chairs that will lift me up here."

Evie laughed. "Maybe so, old man."

"So, how are you doing? I feel like we haven't gotten to talk in ages. The adventure center has been so busy."

Evie broke eye contact and looked back at the mountains. "I'm fine."

"Evie…"

"What?"

"I know you well enough to know that you don't come up here and stare off into the distance unless something's wrong. You aren't even wearing your headphones."

"So?"

"If a teenager isn't listening to music or a podcast, something is wrong."

She giggled. "Oh, is that right?"

He nodded and crossed his arms. "It's the law. Now, what's going on?"

She sighed. "If I tell you, do you promise not to tell my mom?"

"You know I can't promise that."

"Then I can't tell you."

"Okay, fine. I promise. But I don't like it."

She sucked in a breath and blew it out slowly. "I'm graduating early."

"How early are we talking?"

"Three weeks. Well, a little less now…"

"And you haven't told your mom because?"

"Because she's going to freak out that I'm leaving for college in the fall."

"Have you been accepted anywhere?"

"Well, no. But I've applied to a few, including UGA."

"Isn't it a bit late to be applying to colleges?"

She shrugged her shoulders. "I figured it was at least worth a try. I think the UGA deadline was January, but maybe somebody will take pity on me."

"You have to tell her now, Evie. Three weeks isn't a lot of time."

She put her hands over her eyes. "I know. I just don't know what to say. She's going to be shocked. And there's so much change with Aunt Mia having her baby soon. I feel bad throwing this on her."

He put his arm around her shoulders. "You're a good kid. She's going to be proud of you. Shocked, of course. Your mother loves you, and she wants you to have a big, bright future."

"I just hate leaving her alone."

He leaned back and threw his hands up. "Um, excuse me! What am I? Chopped liver?"

She crinkled her nose and cocked her head to the side. "Gross. What does that even mean?"

He waved his hand. "Never mind. I'm here for your mom. And your Aunt Mia is here. She has an entire support system. She would never expect you to stay and take care of her. She's the mom. I'd better go eat my lunch and get back to work at the center," he said, turning toward the ladder.

"I'll talk to her today. I just have to figure out the words."

"Well, figure them out fast, kid. The sooner the better."

Travis loved eating lunch in the square. Since Mia
was busy with paperwork, she'd told him to go have
some time to himself. Pretty soon, that would be a
thing of the past. He'd be a father, and life as he
knew it would forever be changed. Quiet mornings
would be replaced with changing diapers. Late
sleeping would be replaced with cat naps to make up
for not sleeping much the night before. And it would
all be worth it to have someone call him Dad.

"Anything else, hon?" the server asked as she
passed by the outdoor bistro table where he was
sitting.

"Maybe a little more sweet tea when you get a
chance?"

"Sure thing."

Travis loved his little town. Living in the Blue
Ridge Mountains gave him peace. All around him
was beauty, and the people were the best you could
find anywhere on earth. He was convinced of it.
Raising his child in his hometown with the woman
of his dreams was more than he could've ever
dreamed.

But he was scared.

There was no way he was going to admit it to
Mia, but he was pretty terrified about becoming a
father. It was like getting hired for a job he had no

training for. How did he know he wasn't going to mess this little child up?

He supposed everybody felt that way before becoming a parent, but it was waking him up at night. Often, Mia was sound asleep in bed next to him while he stared at the ceiling.

How would he support his family? What if the adventure center stopped making money? How would he give his family enough time and not work so much?

What kind of child would he raise? Would he be strict or too lenient?

There were so many questions in his mind that never went away. His whole lunch had been consumed with worrying about whether they were having a boy or a girl, and whether he would be a different kind of father, depending on the child's gender.

If they had a girl, would he be over protective and drive all of her future boyfriends away?

If they had a son, how would he raise him to become a good man? A southern gentleman who would always give up his seat for a woman and open doors for people.

Of course, all of this was a bit premature, given that the baby hadn't even been born yet.

"Is this seat taken?" He looked up to see an older man standing in front of him, pointing at the chair

across from him. Travis hadn't even noticed that
every other seat in the courtyard was full. The man,
who was using a cane, was holding a plate with a
sandwich on it.

"Feel free," Travis said, smiling. Although he
really wanted to eat lunch alone, there was no way
he was going to tell this man, who was wearing a
veteran baseball cap, that he couldn't sit there.

The man grunted as he sat down and then set his
plate on the table. He leaned his cane against the
black wrought iron and took a sip of his tea. "Getting old is not for the faint of heart," he said,
chuckling.

"You aren't old," Travis said, trying to pay him a
compliment even though the man definitely looked
old. He was the epitome of an old time southern
man with his plaid flannel shirt and denim overalls.
It was late spring and pretty warm, but the man was
quite frail and obviously chilly.

He smiled. "That's okay. You don't have to say I'm
not old. I'm thrilled to be old. By the way, I'm Frank."

Travis reached across the table and shook his
hand. "Travis. Nice to meet you."

"You too," he said before taking a bite of his sandwich. "Eating alone today, huh?"

"Yes, sir. My wife is in the final stages of pregnancy, so she's not excited about coming out to eat."

"Oh, I remember those days. My wife, Irene -

God rest her soul - didn't enjoy those last weeks either. She was awfully uncomfortable."

"How many kids did you have?"

"Five, but only three survived. Two died at birth."

Travis's stomach knotted up. "Wow, I'm so sorry."

"It was an awful thing back when it happened, but I know my kids are in heaven. I'll meet them one day soon, and it will be a wonderful day."

Travis believed in God too, but he often marveled at people like Frank who had such faith. "Can I ask you something, since you have so much experience?"

Frank chuckled. "Experience is just a code word for old."

"No, sir. I didn't mean it like that at all…"

"Relax, son. Being old is a blessing. Many people don't make to to my age. My wife didn't. She died at sixty years old. I'm blessed every day I wake up on this side of the ground. Now, what's your question?"

"Did you ever question whether you'd be a good father?"

He thought for a moment. "I can't rightly say I did, no."

"Oh." That didn't make Travis feel better.

"Don't let that discourage you, though. I've always been what one might call a cocky sort of guy. Didn't even occur to me to be worried about a thing like that. I just assumed I'd be a great father."

"And you were?"

He crunched down on a potato chip. "Nope. I was horrible."

Travis choked on his tea. "What?"

"When we had our first baby, Heather, I was awful. Just dreadful. Worked all the time. I sold insurance in those days, and I left my poor wife to handle everything. You know, men weren't so involved in the raising of kids back in those days. Things were very different back then."

"But you got better?"

He chuckled. "I like to think so. Eventually. By the time our third, Mark, came along, I'd learned that my wife needed help, and I needed to know my kids. I volunteered to coach tee ball, and I even took my oldest daughter to one of those father-daughter dances. I can't dance worth a flip, but she had fun."

"I'm afraid I'm going to make the wrong choices for my child and screw him or her up."

Frank smiled. "Parents screw their kids up in their own special ways. That's why therapists have jobs, you know."

That made Travis laugh out loud. "I guess you're right."

"There are no perfect parents, but there are a bunch of good ones who try hard. Be the second one. Perfect is boring."

"I guess you're right."

"Old people are wise, didn't you know that? We're always right."

"Seems that way," Travis said, laughing.

"Listen, if I can give you one piece of advice, it'd be to take care of your wife. Help her. Do more than she asks and twice what she needs. Your child will see that and learn how to be a good person just from that."

"You know, that's great advice."

"Here's your check, Frank," the server said, laying it on the table next to his place. Travis reached across and took it.

"This one's on me."

Evie was nervous. She had to tell her mother about early graduation this morning. Honestly. She didn't know why she was so anxious about it. While her mom would probably be freaked out a bit, she'd figure it out. She always figured things out.

She walked down the stairs and heard her mom in the kitchen talking to one of the guests. They were chatting over coffee from the sound of it, and Evie didn't want to interrupt. She tried to sneak out the front door, but her mom saw her.

"Evie! Don't you try to sneak out of here without even saying good morning."

She turned around, a smile plastered on her face. "Sorry. Just didn't want to interrupt." Evie walked to the kitchen, dropping her backpack on the sofa as she went.

"You remember Mrs. Drayton, don't you? She and her late husband stayed with us last fall during the pumpkin festival."

Evie looked at the older woman and smiled. "Of course. Your husband carved the pumpkin with the vampire face, right?"

Mrs. Drayton laughed. "Oh, yes. Walter loved vampires. It was such a weird obsession of his."

"I was sorry to hear that he passed away," Evie said. From what she could remember, Mr. Drayton had died of a heart attack just after Christmas.

"Thank you, dear. Unfortunately, our time on earth is limited. If I can give you a piece of old lady advice, it would be to spend as much time as possible with your family and those you love. You never know when it will be the last time."

Evie's stomach twisted into a knot like one of those pretzels she loved at the fair. How could she leave her mom like this? Of course, it was the natural order of things that a child would grow up and leave, but it felt wrong.

"Well, I'd better head to school," Evie said, trying her best to get out of there. "Nice to see you again!"

She hurried toward the door and stepped out

onto the porch, thankful she'd avoided telling her mother one more time. She felt horrible keeping the secret, but she would not tell her in front of a guest either.

"Evie, what's the rush?" Kate asked, following her out the door. "Is everything okay?"

Now was her chance.

"Everything's fine. I just want to get there early so I can talk to my English teacher about our final essay."

Big. Fat. Lie.

"Oh, well, have a good day then," Kate said, giving her a quick kiss on the forehead before she went back inside the house.

As Evie walked to her car, she felt her eyes welling with tears. It was going to be really hard leaving Sweet Tea B&B and her mother.

Mia stood in the living room, an old photo album in her hand. This was one of her favorites, with pictures of her and her mother from many years ago. She ran her finger across a picture from Easter when she was about ten years old. Her mother had made her a frilly pink dress with white lace around the edges. She held an overflowing basket full of brightly colored eggs.

Her mother had truly been one of a kind. Sometimes, she worried she wouldn't measure up. It was only now that she thought about all the things her mother had done for her growing up. Being room mother at the school. Going on field trips. Taking her and her friends on fun adventures. Making sure she had new clothes every year for school. Making holidays warm and wonderful.

How would she ever do the same for her child?

She closed the photo album and held it to her chest, taking in a deep breath. It was painful to think her mother wouldn't be there when her baby was born. It was sad to think how she'd never be a "granny".

Wallowing in her sadness, she set the album back on the shelf and then slid onto the sofa. Feeling like a beached whale wasn't helping her mental state. Being petite and small her whole life, she'd assumed she'd be one of those cute pregnant women who hardly gained weight and didn't even look pregnant from behind.

She was not.

"You okay, dear?"

Mia cocked her head backward to see Mrs. Drayton standing at the bottom of the stairs. She tried to sit up a bit, but it was futile.

"Mind helping me?" Mia asked, reaching out her hand.

Mrs. Drayton laughed and walked to the front of the couch, pulling Mia's hand forward. She was an older woman, but she still had a lot of strength. Mia positioned herself and sighed.

"These last weeks are hard. I remember." Mrs. Drayton sat down in the armchair nearby and gave her one of those grandmotherly smiles her own child would miss.

"Yes, I feel like I might pop at any moment. How does our skin stretch this much?"

"One of those mysteries of life, I suppose. I saw you holding that photo album as I was walking down the stairs. Your mom?"

Mia smiled sadly. "How'd you know?"

"I lost my momma before I had my first child, too. I know what that feels like."

"You do?"

"Of course! Becoming a mother is scary and exciting at the same time. You're sure you won't know what you're doing, and you need your mom. It's a void that can't be filled."

"So, what did you do?"

"Well, I asked other women around me when I had questions. I wasn't afraid to ask for help. And I grieved in those moments that I needed to grieve. You never stop missing your momma. Time doesn't heal. It just helps you learn to deal with it."

"Very true. Thanks for the advice."

Mrs. Drayton stood up. "Well, I'm heading off to town. Can I bring you anything?"

"No, thanks."

"Okay then. I'll see you later."

Mia watched her walk out the door and then closed her eyes, picturing her momma. She missed her so. Each day, her ability to feel her got a little harder. Sometimes, she worried she wouldn't be able to hear her voice in her head anymore. Wouldn't be able to smell her perfume in the air. Every day, she seemed to lose her mom a little bit more, and it was awful.

CHAPTER 3

TRAVIS STARED DOWN THE HILL. "DO YOU THINK WE'VE got enough of those cross ties?"

Cooper looked over at the stack. "I think so. If anything, I think we might've bought too much."

"What about the railroad spikes? Did we get enough of those?"

"What's with you, man? You seem very unsure of yourself today."

Travis sighed and leaned his shoulder against a tree. "Well, I spent most of last night staring at the ceiling worrying about how I was going to send my kid to college."

Cooper laughed as he put on his pair of work gloves. "Aren't you getting a little ahead of yourself?"

"Listen, you've never been a father. These are the types of things that consume your mind every day.

The other day, I worried that I wouldn't see my kid enough if I worked. I toyed with the idea of taking one of those work at home jobs where you answer the phone and take orders."

Cooper slapped him on the back. "You're going to be fine. I'm sure every man and woman goes through this when they have a kid. Thankfully, I will never have to worry about that."

"You don't think you and Kate will have kids?"

"I don't think so. Her daughter is almost an adult. I don't see Kate wanting to start over, and I'm okay with that. It'll give us time to travel and enjoy each other."

Travis's eyes widened. "Oh no! When we have a kid, we won't be able to travel. Mia wanted to see so many places."

"I think they allow children on airplanes these days, Travis," Cooper joked.

"Excuse me?"

The two of them turned around and saw a man standing there wearing a suit and holding a cell phone in one hand and car keys in the other. Travis looked behind him and saw a black BMW.

"Are you lost?" Travis didn't mean to sound rude. It just seemed like this guy was not ready to do any kind of adventure.

The man smiled. "I don't think so. This is the adventure center, right?"

"It is. I'm Cooper, and this is my partner, Travis."

"*Business* partner. You have to start specifying that I'm your *business* partner," Travis whispered through gritted teeth.

"I'm John Creighton. My company produces a reality show."

"What can we help you with?" Travis asked, unsure of why this man was standing on their property in his fancy suit.

"Listen, I'm just going to cut to the chase. Our reality show involves a lot of adventurous challenges. We were supposed to shoot about fifty miles from here, but the place didn't give us factual information about their financial status."

"Sir, I'm very confused. Why are you here?" Cooper asked, a hint of annoyance in his voice.

"I'm not explaining myself very well. The long and the short of it is that the place we were going to use for our show is no longer available. Actually, they got foreclosed, but that's neither here nor there."

"We're trying to get some work done, so if you can just get to the point..." Travis said.

"We'd like to rent your place for the next month so that we can shoot the reality show here. Of course, we'll also give you credits on-screen to hopefully help bring in more business for you."

Travis stared at him for a moment, unsure if he

was offering him the best deal ever or was some kind of lunatic. A reality show? What does that even mean? Travis didn't watch much TV, so he didn't really understand what this man was getting at.

"Listen, we're going into our busiest time of the year…"

"I understand. And to be honest, we're in a pickle here. We will pay you double what you would normally make over the next month. As long as you can show me your books to prove income, we'll pay for it. We're in a bind, and we stand to lose millions if we can't find a place and get started immediately."

"Immediately?" Cooper said, his eyes wide. "We're in the middle of some additions and renovations, like this staircase down to the canyon."

John leaned over and looked down. "I really hate heights."

Travis looked at him and cocked his head to the side. "And you host a reality adventure show?"

John shook his head. "No, I *produce* a reality adventure show. That's very different. I'm not typically on set. I have directors, show runners, and a host for that. And some amazing, courageous camera people."

"Look, we really appreciate you coming by and considering us, but we don't want to do our customers that way. We have people planning trips to come here, and we can't close the place down to the public for that long," Cooper said.

Travis agreed with him, but a part of him really wanted to say yes. Getting double what they would normally make during that month was something they could definitely use. The adventure center was doing well, but they weren't making a profit yet. With a baby on the way, that much extra money would make a huge difference.

"You have a big place here. Maybe we could just cordon off a certain area?"

Travis looked at Cooper. "What about the east side of the property? We haven't put up any zip lines over there, but there's lots of rough terrain. And then there's the big clearing in the valley. Maybe they could use that?"

John held up his hands. "Look, we're not picky at this point. I'd love to go take a peek at the area and see if it might work."

Cooper nodded. "Okay, but just so you know, we will not close the rest of the adventure center. And we will expect to be paid appropriately, even for that area."

He nodded. "Listen, I'm from Hollywood, where everything is expensive. We don't mind paying if you can help us out."

"Great. Let's hop on the UTV and go take a look," Travis said.

Kate walked through the grocery store, absentmindedly grabbing things. She had forgotten her list at home. It was still stuck on the refrigerator with a magnet shaped like the state of Georgia.

Even though she had the fanciest, most updated phone, she couldn't bring herself to use an app to make a grocery list. She always had to write it down. Sometimes, she even wrote it down and then took a picture of it just so she could look at it on her phone when she got to the grocery store in case she forgot it.

Today, as it turned out, she forgot to even take the picture.

Her mind was all over the place. The idea of this big business deal was overwhelming to her. Talia Simon would be in town the next day, and this might be one of the biggest meetings she would ever have in her life.

What if she screwed it up? She was the face and head of the company. Her sister mostly handled the B&B. Mia did a great job with that. They were always in profit. But the honey business had been in and out of profit since it began.

Kate felt like that was understandable since it was a pretty new business, and the B&B had been around for many years. But she still felt like it was her responsibility to make sure she pulled her share of the weight.

She reached up and grabbed a can of marinara sauce, but then it slipped out of her hand and shattered all over the ground. The sound was as loud as a sonic boom, and one of the grocery store workers came running.

"Are you okay?" the young man asked.

Kate put her hand over her eyes. "I'm fine. I'm so sorry! It just slipped right out of my hand."

Another worker came with a mop and bucket. Other shoppers were staring at her, and she desperately wanted to crawl under her shopping cart and get into the fetal position.

"No worries, ma'am. This kind of stuff happens all the time. Just watch out for any broken glass."

She watched as they cleaned it up, unsure of what to do. Was she supposed to get down on her hands and knees and help them? Was she supposed to wait until it was cleaned up before she walked away? Mainly, she wanted to back up slowly until she was around the corner, leave her cart, and run to her car.

"Again, I'm so sorry. I can pay for that."

She hadn't realized that the manager had walked up as well. "Don't worry about it. Accidents happen. We expect it." The man reached up onto the shelf and handed her a jar of marinara. "Here you go."

Kate felt like she was going to burst into tears.

She was having such a rough day being in her own head, and it was always reassuring when people were nice to her during times like this.

"Thank you so much." She slowly walked away, getting to the next aisle full of canned goods before she let out a breath. Normally, she was pretty unflappable. Today, she just felt antsy. Anxious. Uneasy about something.

She thought it was about the conversation with Talia Simon, but that was supposed to be a good thing. It was an opportunity. It was a positive. There was just something in her gut that didn't feel right, but she didn't think it was the potential business deal.

"Kate?"

She turned to see one of Evie's teachers standing behind her. Karen Palmer was Evie's English teacher, and she had always been very kind to her daughter.

"Oh, hey, Karen."

"I saw your little mishap over there. That happened to me once with a bottle of spaghetti sauce. I wanted to dive into the nearest shopping cart and get the heck out of here."

Kate laughed. "Yeah, that was rather embarrassing."

"Well, you must be excited right now. Were you surprised to hear the news?"

She stared at her for a moment before realizing that maybe Mia had told Evie about the grocery store deal and it had somehow made its way to Karen's classroom.

"I was very surprised. I had no idea that was even a possibility. I guess you just never know when opportunities are going to come your way."

Karen smiled. "Well, I have to say I thought it was going to be a real shock to you. I'm glad you're dealing with it so well." She turned and took a can of English peas from the shelf and put it in her cart.

"I mean, it could be a great thing for our company."

She turned back to Kate and furrowed her eyebrows. "I don't understand. How is Evie graduating early going to help your company?"

Kate's heart felt like it stopped in her chest. Evie was graduating early? What did that even mean? Graduation was less than three weeks away, but she didn't graduate for an entire year.

"Excuse me?"

"Evie graduating early. I had to let her out of class yesterday just so she could get fitted for her gown. She's just so excited. Do you remember what it was like to be that age?" Karen said, beaming. Kate continued to stare at her in confusion. As she did, Karen's expression changed to one of regret. "Wait.

You didn't know Evie was graduating with this year's class?"

Kate shook her head slowly. "No, I did not. No one from the school has called me."

"I'm sure they just expected that Evie was going to tell you. She tested out of senior year. They gave her the option to graduate early, and she took it."

Kate couldn't believe what she was hearing. Why hadn't her daughter told her? Graduating was a big event, and she knew Evie had to be excited. Had she been so wrapped up in her own petty worries that she hadn't given her daughter a chance to tell her?

"I can't believe this. I thought I had an entire year with her."

Karen reached out and rubbed Kate's arm. "I'm so sorry. I really thought you knew."

"It's okay. Somebody had to tell me. I just wish it had been my daughter."

Mia wasn't feeling herself, but dinner still needed to be prepared. She was exhausted, more so than usual. Travis and Cooper were on their way from the adventure center to eat dinner with her, Kate, and Evie.

She worried about how her sister was going to react when she found out that Evie was graduating a year early. Kate had been awfully emotional lately, at times even more so than a very hormonal Mia.

"How are the mashed potatoes coming along?" Kate asked. She'd been very quiet since coming home from the grocery store, and Mia knew enough about her sister not to ask. She would tell her when she was ready.

"Creamy as always. Momma used to tell me we did not make lumpy mashed potatoes around here. That was a rule."

"Well, she's right. I love creamy mashed potatoes."

"Where is Evie?"

"I'm not sure. I guess staying a little late after school. I'll text her and make sure she knows to be back in time for dinner."

As if on cue, the front door opened and Evie walked through, dropping her backpack at the end of the sofa.

"Young lady, hang that on the hook by the door. We have guests staying with us," Mia called.

Because their family had grown so much, Mia had started feeding the guests dinner later in the evening. The family would eat, and then an hour later she would heat up dinner for the guests. They all ate the same thing, but there wasn't room for everybody to sit around the same table.

"Yes, ma'am. Sorry about that." Evie hung her

backpack on the hook and walked into the kitchen. "What are we having?

"Country fried steak, mashed potatoes, and biscuits," Mia said wearily.

"You seem exhausted, Aunt Mia," Evie said, squeezing her shoulders from behind.

"I am very tired, sweetie. One day, when you have babies, you'll understand. Growing another human being really takes it out of you," she said, laughing.

"I'm going to go wash up, and then I'll help set the table," Evie said, trotting towards the stairs. Mia watched her sister follow Evie's movements.

"Are you okay?"

"I'm fine, why do you ask?" Kate said, looking down at the biscuits.

"You've been really quiet since you came back from the store. Did something happen?"

Kate tilted her eyes over at her sister. "I don't want to talk about it."

"Understood."

Travis and Cooper came through the front door, loud as ever. Travis made his way to Mia, kissed her on the forehead, and then leaned down and kissed her stomach.

Cooper walked over and hugged Kate from behind, pressing his lips to her neck.

"How are our favorite ladies?" Cooper asked, in his normally peppy tone. Kate forced a smile.

"We're good. Hope you guys are hungry."

Travis let out a loud laugh. "We're always hungry!"

Eventually, Evie made her way back downstairs, and everybody gathered around the table. First, Mia talked about her most recent doctor appointment, and she talked about some things she needed to get for the nursery.

Kate talked about the new guest coming the next day and how she might sign a big grocery store deal for Sweet Charlene's.

Then Travis and Cooper started smiling like two Cheshire cats.

"What's up with you guys?" Mia asked, squinting her eyes.

"Well, we have some big news."

"Very unexpected news," Travis added.

"Well, what is it?" Kate asked, sounding a little annoyed.

"This guy shows up at the adventure center today. Turns out he's some bigwig Hollywood producer. They have a reality show that features all of these crazy physical challenges. Anyway, the place they had booked to shoot the show backed out at the last minute. They offered us an amazing deal to use the east part of the property that we aren't even using. They're going to be there for a whole month, and the amount they're paying us is twice as much as

what we make on the entire property in a month!"
Cooper said it all in one long breath, and then finally
sucked in another breath.

"What? Are you serious?" Mia said, her eyes
wide and her fork dangling in midair with one
rogue glob of mashed potatoes flopping onto her
plate.

"Totally serious. Can you imagine how much that
extra money is going to help all of us?" Travis said,
grinning from ear to ear.

Mia was so thankful. Money was often tight, and
this was going to be such a blessing to all of them.

"Kate, what do you think?" Cooper asked,
smiling.

"I think it's great. Congratulations, guys."

He stared at her for a moment. "Well, I have to
say that wasn't the response I was expecting."

"Oh? What kind of response were you
expecting?"

"Excitement?"

She put down her fork. "I'm sorry. I should have
been more animated. Maybe danced on the table?"

"Kate! What is wrong with you? The guys are
excited, and they should be." Mia chided.

She sighed. " I'm sorry, everyone. I'm excited. I
really am. I'm just having a very hard day."

"What's going on?" Evie finally asked.

Kate laughed under her breath. "What's going on?

Maybe it's the fact that I was at the grocery store, and I ran into your English teacher."

"So? I have a good grade in English. She loves me."

"She does love you. She loves you so much that she was super excited about you graduating in less than three weeks."

Silence hung over the room like an uncomfortable and awkward guest. Mia couldn't make eye contact with her sister.

"Mom, I'm sorry. I was going to tell you…"

"Oh, you were going to tell me? When? After you graduated? After you went off to college?"

Evie put her head in her hands. "I just didn't know how to tell you. I knew you would be upset. You don't want me to leave."

Kate shook her head. "Of course I don't want you to leave. You're my daughter, my only child. No mother wants their child to leave. But it's a fact of life. I know it's going to happen. What bothers me is that you couldn't trust me enough to tell me."

"I'm sorry. I just didn't want to upset you. I couldn't find the words. I told Aunt Mia and Cooper that I was going to tell you tonight."

She turned her gaze to her sister and then to Cooper. "The two of you knew and didn't tell me?"

"Kate, I didn't feel like it was my place…" Mia said.

"Not your place? You're my sister!"

"Now, Kate, don't yell at her…" Travis said, being protective of this wife.

"And you? How could you not tell me?"

Cooper crossed his arms. "Evie asked me not to tell you. She promised she was going to tell you soon."

"Mom, stop blaming them! If you want to blame somebody, blame me! I have homework," she said, pushing away from the table and stomping up the stairs.

Kate said nothing else and walked upstairs behind her.

CHAPTER 4

KATE FELT LIKE THE WORST MOTHER IN THE WORLD. Here her daughter had this exciting news that was such a big deal for her, and Kate had acted like a jerk at the dinner table in front of everyone.

She stood outside of Evie's door, knocking for the third time. "Honey, please let me in. I'm so sorry. I was just in shock."

Nothing. Complete silence.

"I know you're mad at me, and you should be, but we need to talk this out. I'm excited for you, Evie."

Nothing.

In desperation, Kate jiggled the handle, and the door opened immediately. It wasn't even locked. Evie's lamp was on, and her car keys were in the little dish beside her door. Her backpack was still downstairs on the hook, which made Kate wonder how she was doing homework. Her bed was made, and her TV was off.

"Evie?" she called as she walked around the door. She opened the door to her closet, expecting to see her in there reading, but she wasn't there. "Evie!" She ran back into the hallway toward the shared bathroom, but Mrs. Lampton walked out with a towel on her head.

"Kate, are you okay, hon?" Mrs. Lampton was a frequent guest as she came to visit her elderly father in the local nursing home.

"Have you seen Evie?"

"Can't say that I have. Is everything all right?"

"I'm not sure," Kate said, running down the hallway and then down the stairs. "Has anybody seen Evie?"

Mia was standing at the kitchen counter. "Not since she left the dinner table. Why?"

"I can't find her. She was supposed to be in her room doing homework."

"Her car is still in the driveway," Travis said, peeking out the window.

Cooper walked over and put his hands on Kate's upper arms. "I'm sure she's fine. You know where she probably is."

The treehouse. Whenever anything upsetting happened, Evie almost always went to the treehouse.

"I'm going over there," Kate said.

"I'll go with you," Cooper replied, following her.

Kate held up her hand. "No. I want to do this alone. I'm still mad at you, by the way."

He nodded. "I'm sure you are."

Kate didn't have time for a long conversation about how it was a terrible thing for him to do to keep such important information from her. She had to find her daughter.

As she ran down the gravel driveway toward the treehouse, she prayed Evie was there. If she wasn't, she didn't know what she would do. It was getting dark, and there were all kinds of dangerous things in the forest.

She got to the bottom of the treehouse ladder and started climbing up. It was impossible to see whether Evie was up there until she got to the top. Sure enough, there her daughter sat, cross-legged, staring out over the mountain range.

"Evie, you scared me to death!"

She looked at her mother like she was crazy. "Why? Where else would I go?"

"You told me you were in your room doing homework," Kate said, finally making her way to the top and sitting down. The older she got, the harder physical activity became. First thing Monday, she was joining a gym.

"Sorry. Just another one of my terrible secrets, I guess."

There was a long moment of silence between them before Kate finally spoke. "I'm sorry for how I reacted at the dinner table. I should've spoken to you in private instead of acting like a child. I'm just under a lot of stress today."

"I know, which is why I didn't want to tell you. I was waiting until your business meeting was over."

"How long have you known?"

"Literally a few days. I had no idea this was a possibility. I'm stressed out too because I don't know what the next step is. I've missed all the college deadlines."

"Oh, honey, I'm sorry. I didn't think about it from your perspective. I just figured you were really excited to get away from me."

Evie looked at her, tears in her eyes. "Are you serious? You're like my best friend, Mom. Of course, if you tell anybody I said that, I will totally deny it."

Kate laughed and put her arm around Evie. "You're my best friend, too. Don't tell Mia I said that."

"It's not that I want to leave. I fully expected to stay another year. But when somebody tells you that you can avoid an entire year of high school, any normal person would do that, right?"

"I would."

"I just needed a little time to figure out how to

tell you. I'm sorry you found out about it the way you did."

"We both made some mistakes. Now we just need to move on and get you to that graduation!"

"And then what? UGA was where I wanted to go, but they've already passed their application date."

"Well, I guess we need to do some thinking to figure it out."

"I'm not even sure the college is the right place for me."

"Really? I thought you were excited about going next year."

"I mean, the experience of living in a dorm would be cool. But I'm not sure what I want to do. I've changed my mind a million times."

Kate laughed. "Everybody changes their mind. When I was your age, I wanted to be a pediatric cardiologist."

Evie laughed. "A pediatric cardiologist? Where did that come from?"

"One of my friend's dads was in that line of work, and they had a huge house, a nice boat, and they went to Disney World three times a year. I figured you needed to be a pediatric cardiologist if you wanted that kind of lifestyle."

"Well, I think that ship has sailed, Mom."

"I think you're right. Then, in my early twenties, I

thought about going into real estate, working on a cruise ship, grooming dogs..."

"Those are all very different things," Evie said, giggling.

"This is the time of your life where you get to choose. The whole world is right in front of you, and you're only limited by your own imagination. Don't be afraid. The choice you make right now may not be where you end up. That's okay. It's okay to try different things. It's okay to fail. This is that time of your life where you're figuring out who you are, and there is no rush."

"Thanks. And for what it's worth, I really am going to miss you no matter where I go. I'll always come home."

Kate smiled and felt a tear trickle down her cheek as she hugged her daughter tightly. Why did life have to change? Why couldn't babies stay small forever? In fact, why couldn't her waist have stayed small forever too?

Mia sat on the sofa while Travis rubbed her aching feet. Even though she was petite in stature, she found her legs and feet getting worn out at the end of the day.

"Dinner was great," Travis said, working out a

knot on the arch of her foot.

"Thank you. Of course, Kate helped. I hope things are going okay with her and Evie."

"I think they are. She texted me and told me they were having a nice chat," Cooper said as he walked into the living room. He plopped down in the armchair next to the fireplace.

"That had to be quite a shock to her system to find out that Evie is graduating early. I can't imagine," Mia said.

"Well, pretty soon we will have our own child to think about. You don't think this little bundle of joy will ever lie to us, do you?" Travis said, laughing.

"Never!"

"Well, I think I'm going to head out. Tell Kate I'll text her later." Cooper stood up to head for the door. Mia attempted to stand up, ready to give him a hug to congratulate him for the big deal he and Travis were going to sign for the adventure center.

As she went to stand, she got a stabbing pain right in the center of her belly. It took her breath away, and she yelped.

"Mia, what's wrong?" Travis said, standing up beside her. She continued holding her stomach tight.

"I don't know. When I went to stand, I got a really bad pain."

"Maybe it was just a muscle?"

"I don't know. This feels weird. Ouch!" Pain shot through her midsection again, only worse this time.

"I hate to ask this question, but do you think it's…" Cooper started to say.

Mia glared at him, her lips pursed and her eyebrows knitted together. "It is not gas this time!"

Cooper held up his hands. "Okay, Okay. I had to ask."

"Do you think you can sit back down?" Travis asked. She shook her head.

"I can barely move. I don't feel the baby kicking anymore. Something is wrong. We need to get to the hospital."

Without another word, Travis ran across the room and grabbed her purse."Let's go."

"Y'all go on to the hospital. I'll tell Kate and Evie what's going on, and I'll bring them in my truck."

Within seconds, Travis carried her out the door, pain shooting through her stomach and lower back with every movement. Mia was terrified. She was so close to having her baby, but it was still too early to give birth safely. She needed to wait at least a few more weeks.

What if something was wrong? What if she was losing her baby? Oh, how she wished it was just gas this time, but she knew better. Something was definitely wrong.

Kate sat stoically in the car, staring straight ahead, trying to keep herself from crying. She was so worried about her sister and the baby.

"I'm sure she'll be fine. The doctors will know exactly what to do," Cooper said. He had spent the entire drive saying positive things while Kate prayed over and over in her mind.

"Aunt Mia is strong. Everything's going to be okay," Evie said, reaching up into the front and rubbing her mother's arm.

"My sister won't survive if something happens to this baby," Kate said, shaking her head.

Cooper reached over and patted her knee. "We can't think like that. We have skilled doctors at this hospital. They'll know what to do."

They rode in silence the rest of the way. When Cooper pulled into the hospital parking lot, Kate had to restrain herself from opening the door and jumping out while the car was still moving.

They parked as close as they could and ran inside. Kate immediately approached the woman at the front desk.

"I'm here to see my sister. Her husband brought her in with pains. She's pregnant."

"Name?"

"Mia Carter. Actually, Mia Norton. She got married not so long ago."

The woman stared at her for a long moment, like she was annoyed by all the extra information. "They've put her in a room in the women's center." The hospital had done a recent renovation, building a huge women's center where women could give birth and have access to things like large tubs and those big exercise balls.

"Can I see her?"

"No, sorry. You're gonna have to wait out here. When her husband comes out, you can go in."

"Are you going to tell me anything? Is she having the baby right now?"

"I'm sorry. I can't give any information."

Kate groaned and walked away, frustrated. She knew the woman was only doing her job, but she really wanted to know what was going on with her sister. Was she okay? Was she having the baby right now? Was the baby okay?

Cooper put his arm around Kate, and they walked over to a small waiting area. "We'll get information soon. I'm sure Travis will come out here when he can."

"I hate this. We missed so much of each other's lives, and I want to be there for her."

He smiled. "I think that's wonderful, honey. But

she has a husband now. You kind of have to allow
him to take care of his wife."

"I'm going to go get a drink. Does anybody want
anything from the vending machine?" Evie asked.

They both shook their heads. "No, but thanks.
Keep your phone on," Kate said.

She watched her daughter walk down the hallway
and turn the corner. How appropriate it was that Mia
was about to have her first child, and Kate was about
to say goodbye to hers. Actually, that sounded a little
morbid. Maybe it wasn't quite as dramatic as that.

"Kate, I'm sorry I didn't tell you about Evie. I
didn't know for very long."

She waved her hand. "That's old news. I'm not
worried about it right now."

"You're not mad at me anymore?"

"No. I understand what happened, and I forgive
you for not telling me immediately. But if my
daughter ever tells you anything again that I should
know…"

"It won't happen again. Even if she tells me what
she's buying you for Christmas, I will immediately
report it."

Kate chuckled. "You know what I mean." They sat
for over an hour, Kate trying to occupy her mind
with anything else. She needed to know how Mia
was, and the waiting was excruciating.

"Hey, guys," Travis said, walking out from a door behind them. Kate immediately stood up, and Cooper followed.

"Is she okay? Is the baby okay?"

"She's fine, and the baby is fine."

"So it *was* gas again?" Cooper asked.

Travis laughed. "No, it wasn't gas. The doctor said that her cervix has shortened more than it should've at this point in the pregnancy. They had to give her some medication to stop the contractions she was having. Her blood pressure is also a bit high. They're going to keep her for observation for a few hours, and then she will go home on bedrest."

"Bedrest? For how long?"

"They would like to keep the baby in for at least another three to four weeks. Mia will need to be on bedrest the whole time."

"Oh, she will not like that at all."

"Trust me, she had some choice words for the doctor about how she had to manage the B&B."

"We're all going to pull together to take up the slack," Kate said. Her level of stress was getting higher by the minute. In just a few hours, she would welcome Talia Simon from the Deacon's grocery store chain to the B&B. She needed to be on her game, and right now she wasn't even sure if she would get any sleep before the meeting.

"Mia knows you have your big meeting in a few

hours. She thought you might want to come see her so you would know she's okay and go home."

"I'm not going home."

"You have to. She'll worry all night if you're sitting out here. She wants that deal with Deacon's to go through. You would do her a favor by going home and getting some sleep."

"I'll make sure she does just that," Cooper said. "Okay, go see your sister, see that she's fine, and let's go home."

She wanted to argue, but she was too tired.

Evie stood over by the vending machines, going for her second snack of the night. Her mom and Cooper said they would go home as soon as her mom finished visiting with Aunt Mia. She had school in the morning, but being a teenager, she was used to getting very little sleep.

"Hey, Evie."

She turned around to see one of her friends from school standing there.

"Sarah, what are you doing here?"

Sarah was super smart and in all the gifted classes. She'd been very nice to Evie since the beginning, and they had become better friends this year.

"My grandma is in the hospital. Her blood sugar got too high."

"Oh no! I hope she's going to be okay?"

"She will. This happens at least once a year. I don't know why she can't stop eating pound cake."

Evie laughed. "I'm here with my aunt. She went into early labor."

"Is she going to be all right?"

"I think so. They should send her home for bed rest in a few hours."

"I heard you're graduating early. I am too."

"That's great. I'm a little nervous. I'm not sure what I'm going to do with my life after I graduate. I wasn't expecting to get out of there a whole year early."

"Yeah, I planned for it. I've known since earlier this year. I got into UGA!"

"Really? That's great. I'm so happy for you. I thought about going there, but I missed the application deadline. I don't know, maybe I'll just do community college for a year and then apply."

"What do you want to major in?"

Evie had been thinking a lot about that. She didn't really know what she wanted to do with her future. So many of her friends at school knew exactly what career fields they wanted to go into, and she didn't have any idea.

"Honestly, I don't know. I just want to do something that makes a difference, you know?"

"What about the medical field?"

Evie scrunched her nose. "I don't think I would want to deal with sick people. Plus, I'm not smart enough to go to medical school."

"You're definitely smart enough. I'm going to be majoring in engineering. Maybe you could look into that?"

"I don't think that's my thing either. I want to do something where every day is different. Something where I'm helping other people. Something where I'm not stuck in an office all day."

Sarah laughed. "Well, that certainly narrows it down."

"Yeah, as you can see, I don't really know what in the world I want to do."

"That's how my brother was. He's five years older than me. When it came time to graduate, he tried a couple of different majors at college and ended up dropping out. Now he's a police officer."

"How does he like it?"

"He loves it. It scares my mother to death, of course."

"Sarah? Your grandmother wants to see you before we leave," a woman said, poking her head out from a doorway. She assumed it was Sarah's mother.

The woman waved and smiled before disappearing again.

"Well, I'd better go see my nana. Good luck with your decision. And I hope everything goes okay with your aunt and the baby."

"Thanks," Evie said, waving as Sarah walked away.

She turned and looked out the window at the night sky. One of the most beautiful things about living in the Blue Ridge Mountains was being able to see the stars. When she looked at the stars, it made her think that anything was possible. She was just a tiny little dot in the universe.

Sometimes she wondered what her life would look like five or ten years from now. Would she be happy? Or would she settle for doing something that other people wanted her to do?

CHAPTER 5

Kate scarfed down the largest cup of coffee she'd ever made. Thank goodness for the oversized coffee mug Cooper had given her for Valentine's Day. It was shaped like a giant heart with two feet, and it held almost a half a pot of coffee. He meant it as a joke, but today it was a necessity.

After a long night at the hospital, Cooper had finally convinced her to go home and get some sleep. They went back to the B&B, and she crashed for a few hours before waking up around four in the morning, unable to go back to sleep. Now it was almost eight, and she was dragging.

"You're going to give yourself a heart arrhythmia," Cooper said as he walked into the kitchen.

"Caffeine is a gift sent from God," she said,

closing her eyes as she took another gulp. "I have to stay alert for this meeting."

Cooper walked up behind her and slid his arms around her waist, resting his chin on her shoulder. "You're going to do great."

She set the mug on the counter and leaned against him. "How can you be so sure?"

He turned her around to face him, his hands on the counter behind her. "Because they contacted *you*. They want to work with you. And also because you're amazing."

Cooper always had a way of bringing her back down to earth. "I think you've got love goggles on," she said, smiling at him.

"I always have love goggles on when I look at you," he said, kissing her on the neck. Kate closed her eyes and enjoyed the moment until she heard a car outside.

"Oh, no! She's early!" She poured out the cup of coffee she'd just made and ran to her purse to grab lipstick. This woman was going to be sorely disappointed when she saw Kate, since she'd seen her with TV makeup on before.

"Honey, calm down. She's just a regular person like you and me."

Kate looked at him, breathless, as she ran around the room straightening pillows. "A regular person who can change our entire financial lives. Now, get out of here. Use the back door."

Cooper feigned being offended. "You want me to go out the back door like some dirty little secret? Well, I never!" He put his hand over his heart and stomped out the door, turning back to give her one more pouty look. Kate couldn't help but laugh.

As soon as Cooper cleared the door, she heard Talia knock on the front door. Kate took in a breath and blew it out before walking over and opening it. As she turned the handle, she felt like she was literally opening the door to her new future. To her family's future.

"Talia, welcome to Sweet Tea B&B," Kate said, smiling.

"Thank you! This place is just beautiful. You must be very proud." Talia was beautiful, with chestnut brown hair, high cheekbones, and a tiny little waist. Kate felt herself sucking hers in as she looked at her.

"We are proud of it, for sure. Come on in!"

Talia came inside, one small tote bag on her shoulder. She looked around and smiled. "So homey. I bet it's beautiful at Christmas."

"Definitely. My sister, Mia, does most of the decorating during the holidays. She does a great job." Kate hated small talk, and this was most assuredly small talk. "Why don't I show you your room, and then we can come back down here and chat?"

"I would love that. It was a long trip."

Kate offered to take her bag, but Talia declined. She walked up the stairs with Talia trailing behind, asking all sorts of questions. At least there weren't any awkward pauses in the conversation.

"Here we are. This is room six, one of our biggest rooms. The closet is over here, and this one has a private bathroom. If you need extra towels, we have a large linen closet in the hallway."

"Thank you so much. If you don't mind, I'm going to freshen up for a few minutes, and then I can meet you downstairs?"

"Absolutely. Take all the time you need."

As Kate left the room, she felt relief that Talia seemed like a nice, normal person. She wasn't sure what she'd been expecting.

Kate went back downstairs and put on a pot of coffee. She also set out some blueberry muffins, just in case Talia was hungry from her travels. She didn't know how long she would be meeting with her, but it was quite possible that they would go to lunch later. Kate hoped she could make a good enough impression to get the deal signed.

"Hope I didn't take too long," Talia said as she came down the stairs. "I smell coffee. Can I hope that is a fresh pot I can steal a cup from?"

Kate smiled and nodded. "Of course. Would you like a blueberry muffin?"

Talia bit her lip. "I shouldn't. I've been on a diet. I recently lost twenty-five pounds. But I don't think I can say no to that blueberry muffin."

"I'm sorry. I didn't mean to tempt you."

Talia waved her hand. "It's fine. You have to enjoy things in life sometimes. Is that a sugar crust on top?"

"Yes. My late mother created this recipe. I never met her, but my sister used to run this B&B with her."

Talia tilted her head. "You never met your mother?"

Kate poured the cup of coffee and slid it across the breakfast bar, pointing to one of the stools so Talia could sit down.

"It's kind of an interesting story. My sister and I only met a couple of years ago. We matched up through an online DNA test site. I didn't know I had a sister."

"I'm sorry. I didn't mean to pry."

"Oh no. It's not a sad story except for the part that I didn't get to meet my mother. But I ended up meeting my father and my sister. I have more family now that I've ever had, and running businesses with my sister is like a dream come true."

"Well, that's great. I was very impressed when I saw you on the news. So the honey company is named after your late mother?"

"Yes, that's right."

"Mind if I try a sample?"

"Absolutely!" Kate reached across the countertop and grabbed a jar of the plain honey. She opened it and retrieved a butter knife from the drawer. "This is just our plain style. We have lots of other flavors, and I'm working on seasonal flavors as well. Fall and Christmas time are very busy for us."

Talia stuck the butter knife into the jar and pulled out a small amount of the honey, brushing it across a piece of her blueberry muffin. She popped the bite into her mouth and then moaned, closing her eyes.

"Oh, my goodness! I always thought honey was just honey. Nothing special about it, but this is actually amazing. What do you do to make it taste so unique?"

"We have a wonderful beekeeper who helps us. I can't wait for you to try some of the other flavors."

"Well, if they're anything like this one, we're going to be building quite a business with you, Kate."

In that moment, she felt a sense of pride she'd never felt before. This business, named after the mother she never met, was thriving. And this opportunity could take it to levels she hadn't ever dreamed of. Her stomach felt like it had a thousand butterflies in it, but it was a good feeling. A proud feeling. She imagined somewhere her mother was smiling.

Mia pulled the covers up over herself and sighed. "So glad to be back home in my own bed."

Travis set her overnight bag on the chair in the corner of their room. "I'm glad our little bundle decided to stay put for now." He sat on the edge of the bed and put his hand on her stomach. "Anything I can get you?"

She yawned. "I just want to sleep, honestly."

"Honey, you need to eat. You haven't eaten since last night."

She scrunched her nose. "Well, would you eat that food?"

"Well, no, but you still need to eat. How about I go downstairs and heat up some leftovers?"

"Okay, fine. See if we have a biscuit and just pour some sawmill gravy on it."

He stood up and saluted her. "Yes, captain!" Mia swatted at him, but missed.

As he walked downstairs, she laid there, staring at the ceiling. How in the world was she going to get the nursery ready if she couldn't even stand up? And she was going to miss Evie's graduation, too!

"Why couldn't you just cooperate?" she whispered to her baby.

She was so relieved that the baby was okay. Going into premature labor was something she wanted to avoid at all costs, so if it meant staying in bed for a few more weeks, she'd do it. Anything for her baby.

Travis had been wonderful at the hospital, keeping her calm even when she wanted to freak out. There was a moment where she was worried that she was going to lose the baby, and she wasn't sure how she would ever recover from something like that.

The truth was that women had miscarriages and stillbirths all the time, and they somehow survived. She just didn't think she was strong enough.

Still, laying in a bed for the next few weeks was going to prove challenging. Mia was an energetic person, always wanting to do something. Now, the doctor had instructed her to take it easy, watch TV, read books, and just basically do anything she could to sit still. That sounded terrible to her.

But she would do it, like mothers always did. Good mothers always did what they had to do for their children. And this was the first thing she needed to do to protect her baby.

She often wondered what kind of parent she would be. She knew Travis had been wondering that about himself. Getting pregnant had given her a whole different perspective about who she wanted to be going forward in her life.

She wanted her baby to understand the gift of

family. She wanted her baby to experience as much love as possible. But most of all, she wanted her baby to feel the strong presence of a good mother, just like she had felt. Even though her own mother was gone, she could still feel her every day. That was how strong her mother's energy had been.

"Okay, I have two piping hot biscuits with globs of sawmill gravy, and I also brought a side of peach cobbler. And, of course, a big glass of sweet tea." He put them the tray across her lap as she laughed. "How did I do?"

She looked up at her husband and smiled. "You did great. Also, I hope you're ready to go on a strict diet plan with me after this baby is born."

Kate and Talia walked around the town square. They had breakfast together, visited the hives, and now it was time for lunch. Kate normally didn't eat this much in a day, but she didn't want to keep Talia from eating.

"So, we have the sandwich shop, the Chinese restaurant, and the pizza shop. Oh, and we just got the place that makes smoothies, although I haven't tried it yet."

Talia laughed. "I've had plenty of smoothies back

home. I think the sandwich shop sounds like a good place."

"Great. It's right over here. Do you want to sit outside?"

"That sounds wonderful."

They walked over to the sandwich shop and picked one of the small bistro tables outside. It overlooked the enormous magnolia tree that sat right in the center of town on the green space of the square.

"I highly recommend the chicken salad. The Rueben is good too."

Talia looked down at her menu. "There's quite a selection here. I'm surprised. It's such a small town."

Kate laughed. "When I came here from Rhode Island, I thought the same thing. I figured I was going to always have to cook at home because these people couldn't possibly have restaurants. It's amazing what we think about a place before we get to experience it."

"You're right. I shouldn't have prejudged it."

"Carter's Hollow has become my home. Everyone here is so wonderful, and people really do help each other. I try to put a lot of that feeling into our honey business. I want people to get a little sense of this place even if they never get to visit it."

"I definitely think more needs to be done on the packaging to let people know. That's something to think about."

"Good idea."

The server came over to the table and took their order. Kate got her usual chicken salad, and Talia ordered a Cuban sandwich. As they waited for the food, Talia reached down and picked up her leather sided briefcase.

"So, I think it's about time we talk business."

Kate felt her insides clinch up. All day there had been a lot of small talk, and now it was time to talk about the big elephant in the room.

"Good. I'm interested in what you have to say."

"Before I made the trip, I talked with some of our management. At first, we wanted to make you an offer to be in our stores."

At first? What had changed? Kate felt uneasy.

"And now?"

Talia smiled slightly. "This is probably going to come as a surprise to you, but please keep an open mind."

"Okay…"

Talia took a file out of her briefcase and laid it on the table in front of her. "We'd like to make you an offer for your company."

Kate cocked her head to the side. "What does that mean? An offer for my company? You want to buy the business?"

"Exactly. Instead of just stocking the honey, we would like to buy the entire business. We have a lot of great plans, and in order to invest that much, we would want to own the business."

Kate felt like she had been punched in the stomach. Her business. The business that was named after her mother. The thing she had started to build a future for her own daughter. They wanted to *buy* it?

"But my business isn't for sale."

"I know you haven't been considering that, and I know it means a lot to you. But I'd like you to take a look at this offer. I think you'll find it very intriguing."

"I don't get this. You're a grocery store chain. Why would you want to own a honey business?"

"We have a lot of branded products. This would just be another in our line. And I feel like we could also get licensing deals with some of the big coffee chains and tea stores."

"And you don't think I could do that on my own?"

She smiled sadly. "I don't. When you work for such a large grocery store chain, you have all kinds of connections. I'm not knocking your business acumen or your talent. I just don't think you could reach as far on your own as we could."

"I don't understand why we can't just do a normal deal. On the phone you said that you were interested in putting our honey in all of your grocery stores."

"And we are. It's just that management has

decided they would like to have one-hundred percent ownership in the company. They have a lot of big plans. Of course, I can't talk about those because of confidentiality."

Kate couldn't believe what she was hearing. A part of her was flattered that the company wanted to buy her out. Another part of her was livid. Angry. Mad.

"I feel like you came on this visit under false pretenses, Talia. We gave you a free room in our B&B thinking that you wanted to be our business partner. It seems we were mistaken." Without thinking, Kate stood up. She laid a twenty-dollar bill on the table. " I'm not trying to be rude, but my sister just got home from spending the night in the hospital in preterm labor. The only reason I left her bedside was because she insisted I come to negotiate this deal."

Talia looked up at her. "Oh, come on, Kate. Don't leave. Please, just look at the contract."

"I'm not interested in the contract. This company means something to me. I never got to know my mother, but every day that I get to run a company with her name on the sign, I feel closer to her. It means nothing to the giant grocery store chain you work for. I thought we had made a genuine friendship today, and that you understood what this company means to me. I'm not willing to give it up."

"I'm sorry you feel that way." Talia took the file folder from the table and slid it back into her briefcase. "And since we seem to be leaving on an unpleasant note, I'll just stay somewhere else tonight. I'm sure there's a hotel around here."

Kate laughed under her breath. "You'd be wrong about that. And we aren't in the business of throwing people out on the street. Feel free to spend the night and soak up the beauty of Sweet Tea B&B. Dinner is at seven o'clock."

As Kate walked away, she felt a little guilty. Mia had told her everything about Southern hospitality, and maybe she wasn't showing any right now. But at the moment, she didn't even care how Talia got back to the B&B. She was so angry that anyone would think she'd be willing to sell her company, but she was even more upset that she had missed seeing her sister come home from the hospital. That was going to be her focus right now.

CHAPTER 6

AS THE DAYS PASSED, MIA GOT MORE AND MORE USED to being waited on hand and foot. Everybody brought her food like she was some kind of animal at the zoo. Occasionally, a guest walked by and just waved at her like she was the main attraction.

Thankfully, she felt her baby moving almost constantly, which gave her the reassurance that everything was okay. She spent a lot of time with her niece watching useless TV, but she was happy to do it since she didn't know how much longer Evie would live there. She wanted to soak up as much time with her as possible.

When Kate told her what had happened with Deacon's, Mia was appalled. These people had basically done a bait and switch on her sister, and Mia was angry about it. If they had just been honest from

the beginning and told Kate that they were interested in buying her company, they could've saved
Kate a lot of angst.

"It's your turn", Kate said, looking down at the
Monopoly board.

"Which one am I again? The thimble?"

Kate laughed. "You're always the thimble.
Nobody else can ever be the thimble."

"Well, I like the thimble," Mia said under her
breath.

"Where is Travis?"

"I think he and Cooper had a shoot for the reality
show today. He said that it's a lot more work than
they bargained for. Apparently, these Hollywood
types have a lot of demands."

"Well, it's also a lot of money. And since I wasn't
able to get the deal together for the grocery store,
we're really depending on it now."

"Don't worry, sis. Everything always works out
just fine. Mama used to say that all the time."

"Well, I sure hope you're both right."

"So, how are you feeling about Evie's graduation
next week?"

Kate sighed and laid down on the bed, staring up
at the ceiling. "My baby isn't a baby anymore."

"That has to be hard."

"You'll get the same experience one day," she said,
pointing at Mia's belly and laughing. "One day, that

baby you've protected for eighteen years suddenly tells you they're leaving and becoming an adult. I mean, the nerve!"

Mia giggled as she rubbed her belly. "Don't say that. This baby is never leaving me."

"I mean, it's a good thing that I've raised a daughter who's independent and ready to fly, but it sure makes my heart break. I'll miss her so much. We've been together, just the two of us, for her whole life."

"It's going to be okay, Kate. It will hurt, but then your relationship with Evie will morph into something new and cool. She'll become your friend one day, more than just your daughter. That's what happened with me and our mama. She was my very best friend, and then she went to heaven and sent me you. My new best friend."

Mia's eyes welled with tears as she said it. Dang pregnancy hormones. But then she saw Kate wiping away a tear, too.

"Why did you have to go say something like that?" Kate asked, laughing.

"I have no control over my emotions right now," Mia said, more tears streaming down her face.

Kate sat up, wiping her face. "Okay, let's get back to this game. I was beating you, and I'm not too sure you weren't distracting me on purpose."

As Evie walked into the school cafeteria, her hands began to shake a bit. The idea she was mulling over in her mind was a big one. Huge. And her family might just freak out if she decided to do it.

All morning, she'd been walking around at the career and college fair her school held every year. She'd spoken to several colleges, some of which were willing to let her enroll late and still start in the fall. She could go to Carter's Hollow Community College to get her basic course credits and then move on to somewhere like UGA or another big university.

She could also enroll at an out-of-state college that was willing to take her as a late application. She'd even looked at several technical schools. The reality was, she didn't really have a career field picked out yet, so it was hard to choose the right place for her.

Suddenly, she felt lost in the world. Nobody could make this decision for her, and she didn't feel mature enough to make it herself. Now, she was basically an adult, and this was a big decision.

"Um, hi," she said, walking up to the table. She'd purposely left this one until the end because she didn't know what to say.

"Hi, ma'am. I'm Sergeant Halton. Are you interested in joining the United States Army?"

She sucked in a deep breath and blew it out quickly. "Yes, I am."

Travis and Cooper stood at the edge of the large field and watched the latest in reality show competitions. Right now, two men were inside of giant, see-through balls. Each team was using their ball to batter the other team's ball. The men inside were strapped in, but being spun all over the place. It was like a game of soccer on a large scale.

"This is the dumbest thing I've ever seen," Travis muttered.

"Dude, be quiet! You don't want John to hear you say that."

"He's already paid us. I don't care if he hears me."

"What's the matter with you?"

He sighed and rubbed one of his eyes. "I'm exhausted. Mia isn't sleeping well, and I'm always worried about her and the baby."

"It will all be over soon, and you'll have that beautiful baby that hopefully looks like Mia."

Travis slapped him on the arm. "Hilarious."

"I'm stressed out, too."

"Oh yeah? And why is that?"

"I've been wracking my brain trying to figure out the best way to propose to Kate. I mean, you did the cool thing with the zip lines, so I can't do that."

"Maybe you can borrow one of their enormous balls and roll into her."

Cooper slapped him back. "Don't be a smart aleck."

"All she cares about is marrying you, Cooper. Don't make it a big production."

"What if she wants a big production?"

"Haven't you ever asked her? I mean, she's your girlfriend. You know her."

He shrugged his shoulders. "We've never talked about a proposal. She only told me once that she thinks those people who propose on baseball game big screens are silly."

"Okay, so maybe it's because they make such a big deal out of it. Maybe she doesn't want an audience."

Cooper groaned. "So what can I do? Propose over dinner? Hide it in her dessert? Possibly cause her to choke?"

Travis chuckled. "I think there are options between proposing in front of thousands of strangers and causing your potential fiancee to die because of a dessert accident."

"Gentlemen, glad to see you," John said, walking up.

"What's up?" Cooper asked.

"Well, how would you feel about being on TV?"

They both stared at him. "What?"

"We need a couple of extras for this next competition. Want to help? You'll get paid a little extra."

"I think I'm good," Travis said, holding up his hand.

"Come on, man! When will we ever be on TV again?" Cooper asked.

"Hopefully never?"

"I really need the help," John said, putting his hands together like he was praying.

Travis sighed. "Okay, fine. But I'm not getting into one of those big balls."

"You did what?" Evie's best friend, Dustin, stared at her.

"I met with an Army recruiter."

"But why? You're not…"

"Not what?" she asked, her eyes squinting.

"Nothing."

"No, please tell me how I'm not Army material, Dustin. I'll shove you right out of this tree!"

He held up his hands. "That's not what I meant. It's just you've never expressed any interest in going into the military, Evie. Where is this coming from?"

"I'm just exploring all of my options."

"And this is at the top of your list?"

She nodded. "Yes, it is. And I'd love to have your support as my best friend."

"My support isn't important. What is your mother going to say?"

Evie bit her bottom lip. "It's not going to go well. She gets worried if I'm five minutes late coming home from a party. I can only imagine how she'll act when I'm deployed in some war zone."

"Why are you doing this? Why not just go to community college, apply to UGA, and wait a year to get there?"

She sighed and leaned back against the rough bark of the tree trunk. "When I was a little girl, I didn't play with dolls. I played with those little green plastic soldiers. My mom thought it was weird, so she slowly took them away from me and replaced them with other things, like brain teaser toys. Not that she didn't support or respect the military. I guess she just thought little girls should play with little girl toys."

"So that means you need to put on a uniform and join the military?"

Evie smiled. "No, but it got me thinking. So, I talked with a friend of mine at school who has a brother who just went through basic training. He let me ask him some questions, and then I talked to the recruiter. I still have to go through testing and all that before anything would happen."

"I know my mother will not understand this, but it's an excellent opportunity for me to serve my country and get a free education. I had no idea how many educational options there were."

"But what happens if you get deployed to some-place dangerous? That's going to crush your mom."

"I'm sure every person who enlists worries about how it's going to affect their family, but people make the sacrifice, anyway. I don't want to hurt my mom or my aunt, but it just feels right to serve my country."

Dustin smiled slightly. "You're going to make me tear up. I'm actually kind of proud of you."

She laughed. "Kind of? What would I have to do to make you really proud of me?"

"Come back alive."

Mia stared at the TV. She was so sick of watching it, but she had little else to do. Her days were spent eating, napping, watching TV, and occasionally reading a book. Her family members would come in and out, trying in vain to keep her occupied. But nothing was going to take her mind off the fact that her baby could be in danger if she did the wrong thing.

Her natural personality wanted her to get out of bed, run down the stairs, greet guests, and cook a good meal. She felt like a terrible hostess for having to stay in bed like this.

"How's my beautiful wife?" Travis asked as he breezed through the door. He came to check on her several times a day, running back-and-forth across Carter's Hollow in his truck. He'd spend an hour or two at the adventure center, helping with guests, and then he would come back to check on her. Then he would go back and work on the reality show, and then he would come back and check on her again.

She knew he had to be exhausted. But he never said a word. He didn't complain. He always came through the door with a smile on his face. She knew he was tired because at the end of the day, he could barely keep his eyes open at dinner, and he was completely passed out by eight o'clock. Very different from the night owl of a husband, as she had always known.

"I'm doing fine. Just lying around like the big water buffalo I am."

He tilted his head and squinted his eyes. "I'm just curious, but why not a regular buffalo? Why add the water?"

She glared at him. "The proper answer was, 'no honey, you don't look like any kind of buffalo'."

He held up his hands. "Don't get mad. It was just a question. So, what have you been up to today?" He sat on the edge of the bed and rubbed one of her feet.

"Well, let's see. First, I ate the breakfast Kate brought to me. I have to teach her how to make a meal because I'm not sure what that was. Then, I tried to read a book, but I fell asleep. Then it was lunchtime. Kate brought me what I think was a bowl of chili, but it had peas in it. Again, we need to have a talk."

Travis couldn't keep a straight face. "You don't think she's feeding that stuff to the guests, do you?"

"I'm sure she is. These people will never want to come back again."

"I'll remind her where the recipe book is. What else have you been doing?"

"I watched some trashy court TV shows. A woman was suing her mother for accidentally peeing on her sofa. It was so enthralling."

Again, Travis started laughing. "I'm sorry. I know you'd rather be doing just about anything else than laying in this bed."

"I know it's what I have to do right now for the baby, but I swear every single minute feels like it's an hour."

"It will all be over soon, and we'll have that sweet little baby in our arms. Then it will be worth it."

"I know you're right. I'm just being ornery."

"Well, then I need to entertain you. I think the real problem is you've been getting poor quality entertainment in here."

She cracked a smile. "What kind of entertainment?"

He rubbed his chin and looked at the ceiling like he was thinking really hard. "Hang on!"

She had no idea what he was up to when he darted into the closet. A few moments later, he came out and then disappeared behind the foot of the bed.

"What on earth are you doing?"

Without another word, his hand shot up with a sock on it. It was one of her favorite red and white striped ones. "I have come to entertain you!" he said in some weird voice she couldn't identify.

" A puppet show with socks? I don't think that's entertainment."

"Another sock popped up. This time it was her blue one with the gray edges. "Don't knock it until you've seen the whole production!" This time, he was using a totally different voice. She wondered if maybe he was doing puppet shows on the side.

Mia couldn't help but laugh at his antics. Travis always had a way of making her feel better. She watched his little show, much of it a mock conversation between Cooper and Kate, and giggled.

"Okay, okay. I've been thoroughly entertained."

"Well, I would like to know what's so funny?" Kate said, appearing in the doorway.

Travis popped up, both socks still on his hands. "Oh, nothing. She just lost these socks on the floor."

"Oh, did she now? You weren't actually doing a puppet show making fun of me and Cooper?"

"Busted!" Mia said, laughing loudly.

"Now, Kate, we can't fight in front of Mia because she's a fragile pregnant woman. I think you just need to let this go," Travis said, standing up and smiling.

Kate crossed her arms and pretended to be mad. "We'll talk about this later."

"I'm sorry your family is falling apart before you're even born," Mia said, rubbing her stomach.

"I need to borrow your husband for a minute."

"Is it so you can strangle him?" she asked.

"I have given it some thought, but right now it's about something else."

"Okay, you can take him for a little while."

Travis walked over and kissed her on the forehead. "I'm going to run back over to the adventure center after I talk to Kate. But I'll be back in time for dinner."

"Okay. Have a good rest of your day," she said,

forcing a smile as the two of them closed the door. Now she was alone again. Even though she didn't enjoy the sock puppet show as much as Travis wanted her to, at least it kept her occupied for a little bit.

Kate had told her to be happy for the extra rest because the baby was going to have her running until it was eighteen years old. She had a hard time imagining that, but she knew it was probably true.

For now, she would turn her TV back on, find another trashy court show, and wait for her new baby to come.

Kate led Travis into one of the empty guest rooms. She quietly shut the door behind them. "Listen, Kate, I know I'm highly attractive, but I'm married to the pregnant woman in the other room."

She laughed and slapped his arm. "Oh, please, you're not my type. Anyway, Evie and I have a little secret. We want to create a whole nursery for the baby without Mia knowing. I know she hasn't been able to do that yet, and you're so busy. I was hoping you might have some input on how she wants it decorated?"

"That's a wonderful thing y'all are doing, but I

have no idea. Since we didn't find out the gender, I don't even know what colors to suggest."

"We were thinking of doing it in forest animals. Maybe neutral tones with yellow and light brown? Owls, deer, that sort of thing."

He smiled. "I think she would really like that. You know she's an animal lover, and she enjoys being in mountains and looking at the different wildlife."

"Great. Then it's settled. Evie and I are going to do some shopping tonight, and then we will lock ourselves in this room and get started. Thankfully, I think the wall color will work, so we shouldn't have to do much other than decorate."

"We haven't even looked for a crib."

"No worries. Dad and Sylvia are coming to Sunday dinner, and they already bought a very nice crib. Here's a picture of it." She pulled out her phone and showed him the picture that Jack had sent in a text message.

"Wow. That's really nice. I'll have to send him a text to say thank you."

"Also, don't forget that Sunday dinner is really just a ruse to have a surprise graduation party for Evie."

"I totally forgot! Thanks for the reminder. Mia told me to go buy a present, so I'll do that after work."

"Okay, well, you'd better get back over there to

help Cooper. And we will get on the nursery tonight."

Travis turned to walk out the door, but then looked back at his sister-in-law. "Can you believe we're going to be parents soon?"

"You and Mia are going to make the best parents ever."

He smiled slightly. "I know she's going to make a great mom. I just hope I'm going to make an equally great dad."

She walked closer to him and rubbed his arm. "None of us are worried about that, Travis. You're going to be fine."

He nodded his head quickly and walked out the door. She looked back at the empty room. Maybe creating a beautiful nursery would take her mind off the failed business deal.

CHAPTER 7

"WHAT DO YOU THINK ABOUT THIS?" EVIE ASKED, holding up a picture with a deer on it. It was standing in a green field with an apple tree in the background.

"It's cute. I think that would fit on the wall just above the changing table. Get that one and the one with the bunny rabbit."

Kate had a shopping cart, or a buggy as Mia called it, that was almost overflowing with items for the nursery. Lamps, bedding, one of those fancy diaper machines. Evie had filled a basket with pacifiers, bottles and all kinds of teething rings. Much of what she had picked out wouldn't even be useful to the baby for several months, but Kate let her do it, anyway.

"Do you think Mia is going to be surprised?"

"I do. She's been so stressed out about not having a nursery when she brings the baby home."

"How do you think it's going to go when we have guests and a baby is crying all night?"

Kate paused for a moment. "I have no idea. Let's cross that bridge when we get to it," she said, laughing.

"Are Grandpa and Grandma coming to dinner tomorrow?"

"They are. We're having fried chicken and mashed potatoes."

"Oh, one of my favorites. I'm going to miss all the home cooking."

"Miss it? Does that mean you've decided about college?"

Evie cleared her throat. "I think I have."

"And what is it?"

She bit her lip like she was trying to keep from saying anything. "I'd rather wait until I have the whole family together."

Kate stared at her for a long moment. "Why?"

"I just have some loose ends to tie up. Then I think it would be fun to announce it to everyone at the same time."

"Well, okay, I guess. You're not going all the way across the country or something, are you?"

Evie flung her arm around her mother's shoulders. "Mom, you have to wait until Sunday dinner."

As Kate watched her walk down the next aisle, tossing a rattle into the basket that was sitting in the crook of her elbow, she worried. She worried about Evie leaving home. She worried about how she was going to handle her daughter being gone. She just worried, because that's what mothers did.

Kate watched as her father and Sylvia got out of the car. Travis and Cooper ran down to help Jack unload the new baby crib for the nursery.

So far, they had kept the nursery a secret from Mia. That was kind of hard to do, given that the room was pretty close to Mia and Travis's room, but she didn't seem to know anything was going on.

Of course, putting together a crib was going to be a lot harder to do without her finding out. Kate would have to think about that later.

"Hello, my beautiful daughter!" Jack said, hugging her as he walked up onto the porch.

"Hey, Dad. Glad y'all could come today."

He leaned in. "I wouldn't miss my granddaughter's graduation party for anything."

Sylvia walked up behind him and hugged Kate. "Good to see you."

Kate smiled. "Good to see you, too."

She was always happy to see her father and

Sylvia. Any amount of family was a blessing to Kate, since she'd never had much growing up. Now, she was always surrounded by people who loved her and cared about what happened in her life.

Today, she was a little antsy because she knew Evie wasn't telling her something. She'd decided about college, and for some reason, she was keeping it to herself until she could announce it in front of the family. That felt very ominous to Kate.

"Where is Mia?" Jack asked.

Kate laughed. "Really, Dad? She's on bedrest. Where do you think she is?"

"So the doctors told her she can't even come down for family dinner?"

"Nope. She's not allowed to move out of that bed unless she's going to the bathroom or to take a bath. And she's about to lose her mind because of it."

Sylvia stuck out her bottom lip. "Poor thing. I can't imagine how frustrating that must be. I'm going to go say hello to her."

"How are you, sweetie?" Jack asked, looking at her with concern on his face.

"I'm doing fine."

"No, you're not. I can tell by the look on your face that something is wrong. Is this about that business deal?"

She sighed. "Not totally. I'm still upset about it. I don't even know why I continue to dwell on it."

"Honey, they lied to you. You should be aggravated. But that's just God's way of telling you that your business needs to go in a different direction."

"I just feel blocked. Like my life isn't going anywhere. The business is stagnant. My daughter is leaving. My relationship is just the same as it was six months ago. I feel like nothing's moving."

She didn't know why she was telling her father all of this. It wasn't his problem, and she didn't like to talk about personal things. *Usually.*

"I've been at those points in my life before. I understand what you mean. But you're young, and things are going to shake loose real soon. You watch what I say."

"My daughter is going to leave me. I should want that for her, but it gives me such pain."

He took her hand and pulled her over to one of the rocking chairs on the front porch. They both sat down, and Jack held her hand as he looked at her.

"I missed out on a lot of years with you girls. I would give anything to go back and have the years you've had with Evie. But you've prepared a strong young woman for the world. She's independent. She's a little bit sassy sometimes," he said, laughing. "She's never going to leave you. She's going to come and go, and she's always going to need you."

"I know. I think I'm just feeling sorry for myself.

I'm watching Mia about to start her family, and I feel like mine is closing up shop."

"Your family isn't ending, Kate. It's just a new chapter. An exciting chapter."

"Thanks, Dad. You actually made me feel a bit better."

He winked at her. "Every little bit counts."

They walked into the house a few moments later and went to the kitchen. Kate still had some loose ends to tie up with the food. Evie was working on the salad, something she typically did. Kate would miss that when she was gone.

"I'm going to make a plate for Mia," Travis said. "I'll probably just eat upstairs with her."

Jack squinted his eyes like he was deep in thought. "How big is that room?"

Mia piled a bunch of pillows behind her in an effort to sit upright. Travis had promised her a big plate of fried chicken and mashed potatoes, and she could hear everybody downstairs already talking. The smell coming from the kitchen was about to send her over the edge.

Normally, she would just have a couple of chicken legs, but he had promised to sneak a breast up, too. Her appetite was out of control these days, but that made sense given the fact that she was growing another human being.

As much as she wished she was downstairs with the family, having a big Sunday dinner and surprising Evie with a graduation party, she knew that her most important job was as a mother. She would lie in that bed until the moment the baby came.

She heard footsteps coming up the hall and had to contain herself from excitement. She was just way too hungry, even though she'd had a big breakfast.

When the door swung open, she was surprised to see Travis and Cooper carrying a long folding table, and Kate following behind them with several chairs on each arm.

"What on earth are y'all doing?"

"We're bringing Sunday dinner to you, my daughter," Jack said, walking through the door and then leaning over to kiss her on the forehead.

"Wait, you're all going to eat in my bedroom?"

Kate laughed. "It was Dad's idea. I think we can all fit in here."

"Y'all are so sweet! I was so sad that I was missing out on Sunday dinner."

"It wouldn't be Sunday dinner without you, Aunt Mia," Evie said, carrying more chairs into the room.

Kate had told her the bed-and-breakfast was empty for a few days before the next guest arrived.

That was a good thing, given that they were making a whole lot of ruckus in the upstairs hallway.

She watched as her family set up two long tables and one small card table. Kate and Evie went back downstairs to retrieve a lot of the food while the men opened the folding chairs and put them around the tables.

Within a few minutes, the entire dinner was set up in her room, which now smelled like fried chicken. She wasn't mad about it. Fried chicken was one of her favorite smells. In fact, if she could've found a candle with that scent, she probably would've bought it.

"I can't believe y'all did this for me," she said, laughing. Travis walked over and put a wooden tray across her lap. It barely fit over her expansive belly.

"We are a family. And if everybody can't be there, it's just not the same."

She smiled up at him, thankful he was her husband and would be the father of her child. She didn't know a better man, and she was feeling particularly blessed that God chose him for her.

"Here you go," Kate said, sliding a plate in front of her. As promised, she had a chicken breast, two chicken legs, and a mound of mashed potatoes. Evie followed behind with a giant biscuit covered in honey butter.

"I can't even imagine what kind of diet I'm going

to have to go on after I have this baby," Mia said, laughing as she took a giant bite out of the biscuit. If there was one thing Southerners knew how to do, it was making good biscuits. Her mama had made the best, and she was thankful to have that recipe.

Everybody made their plates and sat down at each of the tables. Mia was happy to interact with the conversations. Even though she was still sitting in her bed, she was included. She would've felt awfully lonely up in that room while her family had a big Sunday dinner.

One thing she had really missed as a kid was family. It had just been her and her mom for so long, and she missed her mother greatly. But the gift of family that had come to her more recently had been the greatest gift of her life.

Getting to know her sister, her niece, and her father had been something she never expected. And each time they had one of these big Sunday dinners, it reminded her that she was surrounded by people who loved her. And they would love her baby.

"Kate, you did a great job with this chicken," Cooper said, taking a bite.

"You really did, sis. Mom would be proud."

Kate smiled. "Thanks, everyone. I followed the recipe very carefully this time."

"Have you made this before?" Jack asked.

Travis laughed out loud. "One day, Kate decided

she was going to make fried chicken. I don't know what she did, but every time you would take a bite, the entire breading would fall off onto the plate. It wouldn't stick to the chicken no matter what."

Kate rolled her eyes. "I still don't know what I did wrong."

"That's not as bad as the time mom tried to make meatballs. It was some recipe she found online where you put rice in the meatballs to thicken them up. The only problem is, she didn't know you were supposed to cook the rice first. They came out looking like little porcupines, and I almost cracked a tooth," Evie said.

Kate reached over and slapped her hand. "That was when we were in Rhode Island. You're not supposed to tell my secrets."

"That's not nearly as bad as what Travis made me eat a few weeks ago."

"Don't tell that story, man," Travis said, looking at Cooper, trying not to laugh.

"What did you make him eat?" Mia asked as she took a sip of her sweet tea.

"You hadn't been feeling well, and we didn't have any leftovers, so I just made us lunch."

"He comes rolling up at the adventure center with this cooler in his hand. I got all excited because I thought it meant we had some leftovers. Instead, he pulls out these sandwiches."

"What's wrong with sandwiches?" Mia asked.

"Well, they had peanut butter, roast beef, and pickles."

Mia almost spit her sweet tea across the room. She covered her mouth and then wiped it with a paper towel. "Travis! Why in the world would you make something like that?"

Travis laughed. "I just thought he needed to broaden his palate. Plus, it was all I could find in the refrigerator."

Everybody laughed. Mia loved these moments where the family was together. For the first time in her life, she knew she would never be alone again. She would miss her mother forever, but in her place were people who cared about her so much that they would bring an entire meal, including tables and chairs, to her bedroom just so that they could spend time with her. Many people weren't that blessed, and she would never take it for granted.

They sat around for over an hour chatting, laughing, and enjoying each other's company. Mia was so thankful that her baby was going to have a family like this. This was the kind of family she had always wanted. Growing up as an only child, there were many lonely times where she wished she had a sibling, or at least a cousin.

When everyone had finished eating, Kate stood up. "So, let's get to the real point of this dinner."

Evie stared up at her, confused. "I thought this was just our regular big family dinner? What's the point?"

Cooper stepped out of the room and then came back with a big sign in his hands that said "Happy Graduation, Evie!" Travis, who had also managed to sneak out of the room, brought a large cake with him that said the same thing as the sign.

"We wanted to honor you for your graduation, but we didn't have a lot of time to plan," Kate said, smiling at her daughter. "But we are all so proud of you for doing well in school. We know you're going to do great." Evie stood up and hugged her tightly.

"Thanks, Mom," she said, sitting back down.

Jack stood up next. "My lovely granddaughter, you are the apple of my eye. I never thought I'd have children, much less grandchildren, but you've been such a blessing to me. I'm beyond proud of you, and I can't wait to see the adventures you go on as an adult."

"Thanks, Grandpa," Evie said, wiping a stray tear away.

For the next half hour, they each took turns telling Evie how much she meant to them and how proud they were. It was a very special moment.

"Well, I guess we had better clean up," Cooper said, standing. Instead, Evie stood up, nervously holding her hands in front of her.

"I'd like to make an announcement, actually."

Mia watched as Kate shifted nervously in her seat. Something was definitely going on that she wasn't aware of.

"Okay. Go ahead." Cooper sat back down, and everybody turned their attention to Evie, who looked uncomfortable under their gaze.

"I… I mean… This is harder than I thought it was going to be."

"It's okay, honey. Just say it," Jack said, reassuringly.

"I know many of you have been asking me what I'm going to do after I graduate. It was as much a shock to me as it was to all of you that I could graduate early. I know it has really been hard for Mom."

"I'm proud of you, Evie. Always," Kate said.

"I know. Thanks. And you all know that I've been looking at colleges, and some of you have been asking me what my choice was going to be. I gave it a lot of thought. I considered staying home and going to community college for the first year. I considered going to college out of state."

"So, what did you choose?" Mia asked, excited to hear what the next step was going to be for her niece.

She sucked in a deep breath and slowly blew it out like she was too scared to say the words. Mia thought it was very odd. Most kids would just be excited to announce what college they were going to. After all, it wasn't like the family had any particular allegiance to one sports team or another.

"I'm not going to college, at least not right now."

She saw Kate swallow hard. "Okay. I mean, a lot of kids choose to take a gap year. As long as you go back, I guess that's fine."

Evie looked down at her feet. It was obvious she wasn't done with her speech. "I will go to college one day, but I'm also not staying home."

Kate chuckled. "Honey, I don't think you realize how expensive it is to go out there and get your first apartment. Even if you have roommates…"

"I'm not going to get an apartment either."

"Okay, you're talking in riddles. What's going on?" Kate asked, a hint of annoyance in her voice.

"I'm enlisting in the United States Army."

A hush fell over the room, like Mia had never heard. Nobody knew what to say. Everybody stared at her like she was speaking a foreign language. When people say that you could hear a pin drop, Mia now understood exactly what that meant. She wished she could stand up and hug her sister, because she knew Kate was full of fear right now.

"What?" was all that Kate could manage to say.

"I know this is a shock, but I spoke with an army recruiter at our college fair, and you can get a lot of your education for free through the army."

"Evie, if this is about paying for college, you know I will help you…"

"It's not just about that, Mom. I don't know what I want to do with my life yet. I've always been so impressed with people who served their country. You know July fourth is one of my favorite holidays because I love patriotic stuff."

"Honey, being patriotic doesn't necessarily mean you're meant to serve in the military. I just don't get where this is coming from."

"It just feels right for me."

"But you could get hurt! Actually, you could get killed! You're just a young girl. You really need to think this through."

Evie's eyes filled with tears. "I've been thinking about this a lot. This is what I want to do."

Kate put her head in her hands. "I just don't even know what to say."

"I'm proud of you, Evie," Jack said suddenly.

Kate pivoted her head and looked at her dad. "Are you serious? You're actually encouraging this? Do you know what could happen to her?"

"I know you're worried, Kate, but Evie has to make her own choices in life. I'm proud of her for making such a grown-up choice, even if it's scary to us."

Kate stood up. "I need a moment alone," she said before rushing out of the room and down the stairs.

Cooper stood up. "Should I go check on her?"

"Leave her be," Mia said. Cooper sat back down.

"I didn't mean to upset her, especially after we had such a great dinner," Evie said, slowly sitting back down. Mia could see her eyes welling with tears even from across the room.

"Being a mama is hard," Mia said. "I mean, I haven't even had my baby yet, and I'm already worrying. Your mom will come around. She just needs a minute."

Evie nodded. "I think I'm going to go to my room for a bit." She quickly slipped out of the room.

Mia could see it from both sides. Kate was worried, as a mother. The military was something she had never expected of her daughter, and she was scared.

And then there was Evie, making a very adult decision but wanting her mother's approval.

As Mia watched everybody clean up from the family dinner, she worried about her sister and her niece. Would they be able to come to an agreement on this, or would Kate be anxious every day while her daughter was off serving her country?

CHAPTER 8

"Hold your end up a little higher," Travis said as he and Cooper tried to maneuver a large railroad tie. They were creating a picnic area near the river, but it wouldn't be open for several more months.

"I think you should just hold your end a little lower," Cooper called back.

They finally made it over to the area and dropped the railroad tie like a hot potato. It shook the ground.

"How many more of those do we have to do?" Travis asked.

"I think at least ten?"

Travis sat down on the edge of a picnic table. "I'm exhausted. Mia kept me up last night. She couldn't get comfortable."

"I was up all night because I can't figure out how to propose to my girlfriend."

Travis laid back on the picnic table and put his hand over his face. "Really? You still can't figure it out?"

"It's a big deal, man!"

"It's only a big deal because you're making it one. Just come from your heart."

"Okay, I've been mulling over this idea. I come to the B&B, I decorate the table out under the gazebo, I set up an amazing catered dinner, and I propose right there."

"Sounds good to me," Travis groaned.

"I'm looking for your real input here!" he said, slapping Travis on the leg.

"I'm giving you real input. Just propose already. If you speak from your heart and quit worrying about all this other extra stuff, she's gonna remember it for the rest of her life."

"That's what I'll do. I'm going to text her right now and invite her to dinner in the backyard. I'll just tell her it's because I know she's been upset about Evie."

"Good plan."

"I guess Mia could go into labor at any time now?"

"Pretty much. The doctors would like to keep the baby in another couple of weeks, but I don't think she can hold out that long. She's driving herself crazy being in that bed."

Cooper chuckled. "Yeah, Mia isn't one to lie around and relax. I guess we'd better get back to it."

Travis groaned. "No."

"No?"

"I'm taking a twenty-minute nap right here on this picnic table, and then we'll talk." He put his arm over his eyes and was snoring within a minute.

Evie stood in the half-finished nursery waiting for her mother. They had to finish it up tonight to surprise Aunt Mia tomorrow.

Ever since dinner, Evie had tried to stay away from her mom. She didn't know what to say to make her feel better, and she was a little angry herself. Even though she knew her mother would be worried about her, she didn't quite expect that reaction.

"Hey." She turned around to see her mother standing in the doorway. She quietly closed it behind her. "Mia's taking a bath, and Travis knows to keep her in there. He said we should be able to put the crib together without her knowing."

"Good." Evie sat down on the floor and started

pulling the pieces out of the box. It was a beautiful white crib that looked almost like a sleigh bed.

Kate sat down next to her, her gaze pointing straight at the floor. "I'm sorry. I should have acted like a mature grown-up at dinner. I was just in shock. I didn't see it coming."

"And I'm sorry I told you in front of a bunch of people. I thought it would be easier to tell everybody at the same time. I think I also thought it would give me some level of protection."

"You shouldn't need protection from your own mother."

"I knew you would be worried and scared. I guess I just hoped you would also be proud of me."

Kate's eyes widened as she looked at her daughter and reached for her hand. "Evie, you are my greatest accomplishment in life. I'm so proud of you. Even when you do things that scare me, and when you inevitably do things I don't agree with, I will always be proud of you."

"Really?"

"Of course! Mothers don't always agree with the decisions their kids make, but that doesn't mean we don't love you."

"But you act like I've decided to join some sort of vigilante biker gang. I'm joining the United States military. I think that's something to be proud of!"

"It absolutely is. Every time I see a service

member, I thank them. I just never thought my daughter would be one. I would feel the same way if you were becoming a police officer. I just don't like the thought of worrying myself sick all the time."

"But, Mom, somebody has to do it. Somebody has to do these types of jobs to protect the country, to protect the communities. Why not me?"

She could see the wheels turning in her mother's brain as she thought about that question. "I guess there's not a reason why it wouldn't be you. One thing you'll learn when you become a mother one day is that you have plans for your kids. You have a certain vision in your mind when you have a baby. Mia probably doesn't realize it yet, but as soon as she looks at the face of her little baby, she's going to have plans. You can't help it."

"What were your plans for me?"

"Oh, the normal stuff. Graduating high school, going off to college, coming to decorate your dorm room. And then, of course, watching you get married one day and have kids of your own."

"I'm still going to do all that stuff, Mom. The military is offering me such great benefits with education. I know you could help me out with that, or I could get loans. But I just want to see what it's like serving my country for a little while. Maybe I'll love it. Maybe I won't. But at least I'll get some training and figure out what direction I want to go in my life."

Kate nodded and smiled slightly. "You're so grown up. How did this happen so quickly?"

"I've been working on it for about eighteen years," Evie said, laughing.

"I am proud of you, honey. And I will be with you every step of the way through this process. I always have your back. No matter what."

"Thanks. I guess we should start working on this crib. Mia can't stay in the bathtub forever."

Cooper stood under the gazebo, all the food laid out on the table in front of him. He lit the candles and waited for Kate to come from inside the house. Tonight, he had gotten the dinner catered by her favorite local restaurant. They were having stuffed mushrooms, a four cheese lasagna, and the best garlic breadsticks he'd ever tasted in his life.

She had asked why they were having such a special dinner, and he told her he knew she was stressed out lately with everything going on. That was the truth. The business deal had really rocked her, and then Mia going into early labor, hearing about Evie going into the military, and working on the nursery. There was just a lot going on in Kate's life, and most of it was adding stress.

He hoped this dinner would give her something happy to think about. A way to look forward to her new future. Evie leaving home, and especially going into the military where she could be in danger, was really doing a number on Kate's mind.

The only thing he knew was he wanted to be her husband forever. There was no one else, and there would never be anyone else. He was more sure about proposing to her than he had been about anything in his whole life.

Over the last few weeks, he'd been spent trying to come up with the perfect speech. The perfect way to ask her to marry him. He wanted it to be memorable. He wanted her to cherish that moment forever.

Even though he would never admit it to Travis, he even looked on the Internet, trying to find the most romantic proposals. This was important, and he would not screw it up.

Kate walked out of the house wearing a long white skirt, a baby blue T-shirt, and her hair pulled up in a ponytail. Even when she wasn't trying to look beautiful, she always did. She had a long, lean body like a ballet dancer, even though she had never danced a day in her life. Most women would probably be jealous of her figure.

"This looks beautiful, Cooper. Thank you so much for doing this. I think I need a night away from all the stuff going on in that house," she said, smiling. He walked over and kissed her on the cheek.

"Have a seat," he said, pulling out her chair.

"You even have candles? Everything looks so nice."

"I'm glad you like it. I got the breadsticks," he said, grinning as he held up the basket.

"Oh, I love the breadsticks. If I only got to eat one thing for the rest of my life, it would be these breadsticks."

"I don't think your digestive system would appreciate that."

Kate laughed. He loved hearing her laugh. It was unique, but not annoying. He wanted to spend the rest of his life making her laugh as much as possible.

"I talked to Evie earlier. We cleared the air. I think everything is going to be fine. I'll still worry, but I'm proud of her."

"She's really becoming an independent young woman."

Kate sighed. "We've basically grown up together. I don't know what I'm going to do without her. Everything is going to be so different."

"Well, you always have me."

She reached across the table and squeezed his hand. "And I'm super thankful for that."

"Plus, we're going to have a new baby in the house."

"We? You don't live here. You won't have to listen to those long nights of crying."

He wanted to tell her he planned to live in the same house with her. Maybe not at the B&B, but at their own house. After all, it would be a little tight for Mia, Travis, Kate and Cooper to all live in one house together. Sometimes there needed to be a little separation, and he had a nice place near the square.

"You know what I mean. A new little baby in the house to play with is going to be something you enjoy."

"I'll enjoy being the aunt. I certainly wouldn't want to be the mother of a baby all over again."

For a long time, Cooper thought he needed to have children. But when he met Kate and Evie, he felt like Evie was his daughter. There was nothing he was missing in that area. One day, Evie would hopefully get married and have children of her own, and then they would have grandchildren.

"Let's dig in," Cooper said, uncovering the lasagna. It was still piping hot, so he cut a piece for Kate and put it on her plate. She scooped out some of the stuffed mushrooms and took two of the breadsticks.

"Everything smells so good. I just love Italian food."

"Care for some wine?"

"Of course!" He poured her a glass of white wine, knowing full well she would probably ask for sweet tea at some point, too. Kate could never get through a meal without sweet tea, even though she had hated it when she first moved there.

"So have you heard anything else from Deacon's?"

She shook her head. "No. I'm kind of bummed about all of it because I had that one opportunity on TV, and I blew it. I wasn't good in the interview, and the one lead I had turned out to want to buy the company."

"You did great on TV. What are you talking about? And it's not your fault that those people tried to do bait and switch on you."

"I guess. I just feel like I'm sort of stuck in my life right now. I'm not moving backward, but I'm not moving forward either. I'm not a person who enjoys just staying in the same place forever."

"Do you mean Carter's Hollow?"

"No, I love it here. I don't think I'll ever want to leave. But I just feel like I'm not making any actual progress. The business is doing fine, but it's not growing. And Mia is going to be so busy with the baby that she'll be lucky to keep the B&B running. I'll have to help her with that. Travis is too busy with the adventure center. I guess I'm just feeling a little overwhelmed. I'm ruining dinner with all this talk."

"You're not ruining anything. You can always come to me with your problems, and I'll do my best to help you. We're a team," he said, winking at her.

"A team, huh? You think we make a good team?"

"I think so," he said, taking a bite of lasagna. "You don't?"

"Actually, I think we make a pretty awesome team."

Now was the time. She had just given him the perfect opening. Even though he had planned to ask her during the dessert, which was tiramisu, he decided to do it now. No time like the present.

"Kate, I want to…"

Before he could finish his sentence, Kate's phone rang. She had set it on the table next to her just in case Mia needed anything, since Travis was away for the evening working on the reality show. Cooper had begged him to let him have the evening to finally propose.

"I'm so sorry. I don't recognize this number. Mind if I answer it right quick?"

Yes, he minded. He minded a lot. But he couldn't tell her that. "Of course. Go ahead."

Kate stood up and walked away from the table. He couldn't quite hear the conversation, but it was pretty animated. When she came back, she was beaming.

"You won't believe who that was!"

"Who?"

"The lady from Deacon's. She talked to the management, and they realized what they were asking was too much. They still want to partner with us. She said that she's emailing me a brand new offer. But they need me to answer quickly because they have to make some decisions on space in the stores. Do you mind if I take a rain check on dinner? We can eat it later tonight on the sofa and just watch trashy TV?" She looked at him hopefully.

Cooper's stomach dropped. He'd wanted to do this tonight, but he would not ruin it by getting into an argument about her leaving dinner, and he certainly would not propose eating leftovers in front of the TV.

"You know what? Dinner can wait. I'll put everything in the fridge, and I'll go help Travis at the center. I'll come back over later, and we can eat together."

She ran over to him and kissed him on the cheek. "Thank you so much! This could be a huge deal. I have to get to my computer!"

As he watched her run back into the house, he sighed. Now he would have to wait for the next opportunity to propose to her, get up his nerve again, and get that ring on her finger somehow.

Travis tied the makeshift blindfold around Mia's head. He was really just using one of his old business ties that he normally reserved for wearing to funerals and church functions.

"Is this really necessary? And I'm also not sure that my doctor would be okay with y'all walking me around with a blindfold over my eyes while I'm hugely pregnant."

Kate took her other arm. "I promise it's for a good reason. We'll get you right back in bed. The doctor doesn't know whether you're walking down the hallway or walking to the bathroom, so I think we can cheat a little."

Mia had no idea what they were up to. She was tired and coming into her last days of pregnancy, or at least she hoped so. Right now, all she wanted to do was nap and eat. Sometimes, she didn't even turn on the TV. She couldn't stay awake long enough. Apparently, pregnancy had also brought on narcolepsy.

"Okay, we're here." Travis stopped her in the middle of the hallway. Mia was so discombobulated at this point that she had no idea which door she was standing in front of. Maybe they were parading her around as the hugely pregnant woman so they could show her to guests like she was some kind of freakish circus sideshow.

"Can I take this thing off my face?"

She heard the door in front of her open, but she couldn't see anything. It was surprising just how well Travis' tie was working to block out light.

Travis took the tie from around her head and allowed her to open her eyes. At first, the light was a bit blinding until her eyes readjusted.

Mia couldn't believe what she was seeing. A completed nursery was right before her eyes. What had once been one of their extra guest rooms that wasn't decorated yet had turned into a beautiful room that was going to be perfect for her new baby. She looked around and saw Travis, Kate, and Evie standing there with smiles on their faces.

"I don't understand. How did y'all do this without me knowing?"

"Well, honey, you do sleep a lot."

Mia laughed, tears streaming down her face as she meandered around the room. There were decals of forest animals all over the walls behind the beautiful white crib. She ran her finger over the wood and looked down into it, noticing brand new sheets on the bed.

There was a changing table, a rocking chair, and a small bookshelf covered with books for kids and stuffed animals. She slowly turned around and looked at Kate.

"Y'all did an amazing job! I couldn't have done it any better."

"Evie helped me a lot. And dad bought the crib."

She walked over and hugged her sister tightly, her enormous belly causing her to stretch her arms a lot further than normal.

Then she hugged her niece. "Thank you for helping, Evie. It really is beautiful."

"Don't forget your husband. He made sure that the surprise wasn't ruined, and he might've kept you in the bathtub a little longer than normal a couple of times."

She looked at him and smiled. "Is that why you wouldn't let me out of the tub the other night? I was turning into a raisin!"

He hugged her tightly and kissed her on top of the head. "A man has to do what a man has to do."

As Mia stood there looking around the nursery and imagining herself sitting in that rocking chair, holding her new baby, she was filled with gratitude for her family.

There were so many things she hadn't been able to do for the baby, but they had stepped up and done it themselves.

"I'm sorry we haven't been able to have a baby shower," Kate said. "It's just with you being on bedrest, I didn't think you'd want a bunch of people in your bedroom."

She shook her head. "You're right about that. I don't feel like having a lot of company right now."

"We'll do something after the baby is born. It'll be more fun once we know the gender, anyway."

"I hate to be a buzz kill, but it's time to get you back in bed," Travis said, putting his arm around her.

"Can't I just stay in here for a little while? Sit in my new rocking chair?"

He shook his head. "No way. Back to bed, lady."

CHAPTER 9

Kate sat in the bleachers at the high school, nervously fiddling with the bracelet on her wrist. Tonight, her daughter was graduating from high school, and she couldn't believe everything had happened so fast.

She still remembered taking Evie to her first day of preschool, and then her first day of kindergarten. Every little milestone had seemed to come quicker and quicker over the years. Before she knew it, her daughter was wearing makeup, driving a car, planning a future on her own. Where had the time gone? So often, she'd wished she could slow it down, but life moved on.

And now, as she watched her sitting in the folding chair on the football field, she wondered what was next. When Evie went off to basic training, how would she let her go? How could she say good-bye? How could she send her little girl out into the cold, often harsh world on her own? It seemed so impossible.

For now, she was trying not to think too far ahead. She just wanted to watch her daughter walk across that stage and get her diploma. It was something her own mother didn't get to see her do, and she would not take it for granted.

"Is that her in the fifth row?" Cooper asked.

"Yes. She's sitting on the end."

He reached over and took her hand. "You know it's going to be okay, right?"

"I know. It's just a lot to take in."

"Well, at least you have the Deacon's deal going again. That's going to be huge."

She nodded and smiled. The phone call she had gotten from Talia was surprising, to say the least. Not only had they decided that they wanted to be in business with her, but they were going to put her in all of their stores immediately. Apparently, management was very impressed by Kate's ability to stand up for herself.

The company had offered to fund some new ventures, as well. They would go into business together in a new dessert company based on a lot of her mother's own recipes. That was also going to bring plenty of business to the B&B. Kate and Mia were very excited.

"I sure wish Mia could've been here in person."

"I do too, but at least she's able to watch it on livestream. Technology is great, isn't it?"

"It is."

"We didn't miss anything, did we?" Jack and Sylvia appeared from behind and quickly sat down next to Kate.

"Nope. They should start any minute."

"I can't believe my granddaughter is graduating today. That's making me feel a bit old."

Kate patted him on the knee. "Don't worry, Dad. You *are* old." He laughed loudly, and other people turned around.

"Very funny. Where's Brandon? Shouldn't he be here for his daughter's graduation?"

"I would normally agree with you, but his wife just had surgery. With the early graduation happening, he couldn't plan around it. He's watching on livestream too."

They chatted for a few moments before the graduation started. First, the school chorus sang a song, and then the principal took to the stage. They all stood for the national anthem before sitting down again.

The principal called out the names of people who

were graduating with honors, and Evie was one of them. She stood up with her gold cord around her neck, waving at her family proudly before she sat back down.

As they called out the name of each graduate, Kate thought about those families and what they had gone through to get their child to that point. Had it been as hard as Evie's journey at some points?

After all, when she had arrived in Carter's Hollow, she was a problem child, always getting in trouble back in Rhode Island. Now, she was graduating with honors and had a bright future ahead of her.

So much had changed since they had arrived at Sweet Tea B&B. They had family, friends, and a safe place to call home. Living out in the woods right by the lake with a view of the Blue Ridge Mountains was like living in heaven on earth.

As the principal called out Evie's name, her whole family stood up and clapped, even though they weren't supposed to do that until the end. Kate couldn't contain herself. She was so proud of her daughter, and this was truly the end of an era. No longer did she have a little kid in school. She had an adult daughter who was going to be her best friend for the rest of her life.

～

Kate was happy to get away for the day. It was very seldom that she and Cooper had an entire day to themselves. So much had happened lately that she felt like a day away would do them both good.

Today they had gone shopping, and Kate had primarily bought baby clothes for Mia's new baby. She felt like she was just as excited to get a new niece or nephew as Mia was about having her first baby.

They were going to have so much fun together, dressing the baby up and watching all the firsts. First word, first steps, first birthday. Sometimes Kate was sad that she didn't get to do that with her sister when she had Evie, but this was like getting a second chance.

After doing some shopping, Cooper had taken her out to lunch at the café. She had her favorite chicken salad with a side of chips and sweet tea. Now she felt like she was about to pop, and she needed to get some exercise.

Cooper suggested they take a short hike up to their favorite vista overlooking the Blue Ridge Mountains. She was game, because she needed that food to get out of her stomach as quickly as possible. As thin as she was, she still felt like she couldn't breathe.

"It's getting really hot out here now," Kate said as they walked.

"Yeah, it's getting to be that time of the year.

People think it doesn't get hot in the mountains, but they would be very wrong about that." The south in general had a reputation for heat and humidity, and the mountains were no different. The summer months could be brutal.

"My favorite is when it's warm outside, but there's a breeze. It's like the best of both worlds."

They continued walking up the last part of the steep incline. Many years ago, somebody had built a very nice, sturdy wooden bench at the top. That was one of their favorite places to sit and stare out over the beautiful mountains.

Kate had never been around mountains until she moved to Sweet Tea B&B. She didn't even know that she liked them until then. One thing she had learned was that the mountains always looked different. You could go and sit in the same spot a hundred times, and you would see a hundred different views.

Sometimes the mountains looked blue, hence their name. Sometimes there was a fog hanging in front of them, so much so that they disappeared completely, as if nothing was there. Other times, there was a bright blue sky above with big white puffy clouds, and the mountains were different shades of green. She especially loved the evening when the sun was sinking below the mountains, casting different levels of light on them.

Having lived there, now she could not imagine

ever going anywhere else. The ocean was beautiful, and she liked to visit, but the mountains were home. They enveloped her like a warm hug.

They sat down on the bench, each of them trying to catch their breath.

"I have got to go to the gym more," Cooper said, laughing. He was in great shape, truth be told, but everyone struggled a little more with their physical fitness the older they got.

"Same here. Maybe I'll start doing some cardio again."

"Want a granola bar?"

"Sure."

He pulled two of them out of his backpack, as well as a bottle of water for each of them. She loved being with Cooper. Their relationship hadn't started out in the best way, but it ended up being one of the greatest blessings of her life.

She didn't know what she would do without him. He kept her sane, and he leveled her out when she was about to spiral out of control. She had a tendency to work herself to death, and she blamed herself for pretty much anything that went wrong in her world. These were qualities she was constantly working on, but never making much progress.

Cooper, on the other hand, was a happy-go-lucky kind of guy. He made people smile, and he made her laugh to the point she felt like she was going to wet her pants. She couldn't imagine sharing her life with anybody else.

"How is Mia doing today?"

"When I left, she was taking one of her numerous daily naps. I left her some snacks and snuck out of there."

"I know she's getting so tired of being pregnant."

"She is. Those last few days of pregnancy are the hardest."

"You know, sometimes I wish we were together when you were pregnant with Evie."

Kate laughed. "I think my ex-husband would've had something to say about that."

He lightly slapped her on the knee. "You know what I mean. I wish we could have started out together and had our own family."

"I do too. But then she wouldn't be Evie because she is part of her father. I'm glad that they have a relationship now, even though it's not as close as the one she has with you."

"You think so?"

"Evie loves you like a father. Like a real father. Like a father that's there every single day of her life to support her. You have to know how much she loves you?"

"I love her, too. As far as I'm concerned, she's my kid."

Kate leaned her head over onto his shoulder. "And that's just another reason I love you so much."

"Do you think we'll be together forever?"

"I hope so," she said. Cooper wasn't often this sentimental. She wondered what was going on. Maybe watching Mia and Travis going through the process of becoming parents was triggering it. Maybe watching Evie go away was making him feel something. After all, he loved her, too.

"I wanted to talk to you about something..."

"Okay."

"I've been thinking a lot about..."

As usual, at the most inopportune moment, her cell phone rang. She pressed the button on the side of it to silence it, wanting to pay attention to what Cooper was saying.

"Sorry. I should've turned my phone off. It's just with Mia..."

"I understand. So what I was saying is that I've been thinking..."

Again, her cell phone rang. This time, Kate looked down at it and noticed that it was Travis's number. "Hello? Travis?"

"Mia... hospital..." The call was cutting in and out because service wasn't great in that area. Kate knew they had to get down the mountain as quickly as possible when she heard the word hospital.

"We have to go. I think Mia is being taken to the

hospital. That was Travis, but the call was cutting in and out."

"Let's go!" Cooper said, grabbing her hand as they started the hike back down the mountain.

"I can't believe that Aunt Mia is down the hall having her baby. What do you think it's going to be?" Evie asked her mother.

"I don't know. She's been carrying kind of low, so I think that means a boy? I don't really keep up with all the old wives' tales."

"Is Travis hoping for a boy?" Evie asked Cooper.

"If he is, he hasn't mentioned it. He's not stupid. Men should keep their mouth shut and never say what gender they're hoping for."

Kate laughed. "Good advice."

"How long have they been back there?"

Kate looked at her phone. "Well, Cooper and I got here about an hour ago, so at least that long. Travis said her water broke about a half an hour before he called us."

Evie had met them at the hospital. She had been in town, hanging out with friends to celebrate their recent graduation.

"I think I'm going to go get something out of the vending machine."

"Evie, didn't you just eat?" Kate asked, laughing.

"I had a salad. That's not an actual meal. I want some chips or something." She stood up and started walking toward the hallway where the vending machines were.

"Hey, wait up. I might want something," Cooper said, chasing after her.

"Get me some of those cheese crackers if they have them," Kate called as Cooper jogged away.

They walked down the hall and turned the corner, now out of sight from Kate. When they got to the vending machine, Evie put in a dollar bill and got some chips.

"Hey, can I talk to you about something right quick?"

She turned and looked at Cooper. "Sure. What's going on?"

He reached into his pocket and pulled out a small blue velvet box. He opened it to reveal the engagement ring he had purchased for Kate.

"Do you think your mother will like this?"

Evie stared at the ring for a long moment and then looked at him. "Are you going to propose to my mom in the middle of the waiting room?"

He scoffed and rolled his eyes. "Of course not! I've been trying to propose to her for over a week now. I keep getting interrupted."

"Interrupted?"

"First by an important business phone call, and then by Mia going into labor. It's like the universe is trying to keep me from proposing."

Evie smiled. "You and my mom are going to get married? That's so cute!"

"I don't know if she's going to marry me, but I would like to at least get to ask. Back to my original question. Do you think she'll like this ring?"

"Of course she's going to like that ring. It's beautiful. And you don't need to go to a bunch of trouble. I know Mom wants to marry you, and it would make me feel a lot better if she had that to focus on when I left. It's going to be so hard for her."

He turned and looked at the vending machine while putting the ring back in his pocket. He found the cheese crackers and pressed the button to retrieve them.

"I just want it to be a memorable proposal. I've been driving myself crazy trying to figure out just how to ask her."

Evie put her hands on both of his shoulders and turned him around to face her. "It doesn't matter how you ask her. She loves you, and she's going to say yes. So just do it. Don't think about it."

"Now?"

Evie laughed. "Okay, maybe not *right now*. That would be kind of silly to do it in the middle of a hospital waiting room while my aunt is giving birth. But pretty much any other time."

Cooper smiled. "You realize this is officially going to make you my stepdaughter?"

"Oh, so I can call you Pops?"

"No, you absolutely cannot call me that."

"Daddy? Pa?"

"We'll work on a name," he said, laughing as they headed back to the waiting room.

Mia had never experienced such pain in her whole life. When the contractions came, it felt like her insides were being ripped out. The doctor said she needed one more centimeter before she could get the epidural, and she was doing every kind of meditation and manifestation she could think of to get that one centimeter moving along.

As she came out the other side of another contraction, Travis held her hand and sat beside her. There wasn't much else he could do. She almost felt sorry for him between contractions when she wasn't wanting to rip his face off for putting her in this condition.

"Is there anything I can do? Anything? Rub your back?" He had been asking these types of questions every few minutes. She could tell he wanted to take her pain away, but that was the great irony of child-birth. He caused her to be pregnant, but there wasn't a thing he could do to help ease her pain.

"Just hold my hand," she said, as she did every time he asked. There really wasn't much else he could do. Just him being beside her, as he always was, made her feel safe.

"Surely the next time they check you, you'll have progressed."

"I hope so. I'm exhausted."

A few minutes later, the doctor came back into the room. She was an older woman with gray hair, but had tons of experience. Out of the practice that Mia went to, she was her favorite.

"Okay, let's check you again, my darlin'. If you haven't progressed, we might have to give you a medication to help you along."

Mia laid there, praying to God that she had progressed another centimeter, as the doctor checked her. There was nothing she wanted more in the world than to hold her sweet baby in her arms right now.

"Well? What's the verdict?" Travis asked when the doctor sat back up. She shook her head.

"I am afraid that we haven't seen much progress. The baby could be stuck in the birth canal, and if that's the case, we may end up doing a C-section."

"I was really hoping to avoid that," Mia said, on

the verge of tears. Something about having a C-section made her feel like a failure of a mother already. She knew that wasn't logical as many had C-sections every single day, and she didn't think lesser of them.

"You're very petite, and if your baby is larger than you can safely give birth to, a C-section is the safest option. Otherwise, your baby can suffer with oxygen deprivation."

"So, what do we need to do?"

"We're going to continue to monitor the baby's vitals for the next half hour, and then we will make a final decision. Just hang in there."

As the doctor left the room, Mia felt devastated and helpless. There was nothing she could do to hurry birth along, and she was starting to fear for her baby's safety. She had loved being petite her whole life, but right now, she was pretty aggravated by it.

"It's going to be okay. You and the baby are going to be fine," Travis said. The way he said it made it sound like he was trying to calm himself down even more so than her. He must have felt more helpless than she did.

"If I have to have a C-section to make sure my baby is healthy, then that's what I'll do. It will be my first act of bravery as a mother."

He smiled. "You're going to be the best mom."

Kate laid her head on Cooper's shoulder as they stared at the TV in the waiting room. Thankfully, it was a quiet night at the hospital, so there were no more families in there with them. Evie had gone home to get some rest and make sure there was food in the house when Mia came home in a couple of days. She'd offered to make some casseroles, so nobody had to worry about cooking for the next few days.

Evie had actually become a good little cook in her time at Sweet Tea B&B. She took great pride in learning her grandmother's recipes, even though she never met her. Being a whiz at southern cooking wasn't something she ever thought she'd say about her daughter, but it was true.

"What are we watching?" Cooper asked, laughing.

"It appears to be a cheesy romance movie. I checked the other channels, and all we had was news and some kind of documentary about a serial killer. I'm really not interested in either of those at the moment."

"Cheesy romance movie, it is then."

They sat quietly watching the movie, and Kate couldn't believe that she was actually getting interested in it. It was about high school sweethearts who were torn apart at some point and came back together when they were in their forties. At the end of the movie, the guy got down on one knee in the middle of a restaurant and proposed to the woman.

"Yuck. I would hate that."

"What?"

"The cliché of somebody proposing in the middle of a fancy dinner. I mean, can't you be more creative than that?"

"You don't think that's romantic?" he asked, looking down at her.

"No, because it's been done a million times. I mean, if he loved her that much, and they had been together since they were teenagers, he should have something unique planned for her. It's like when those people propose at baseball games. I hate that too."

"What do you think is romantic, then?"

"I don't know. I don't have anything in mind. I just know what I don't like," she said, laughing. "Or maybe I'm just tired and ornery."

"Hey, y'all." They both looked up to see Travis standing in the doorway of the waiting room. Kate jumped up.

"Well? What do we have?"

"We have a baby stuck in the birth canal, and a mother getting prepped for a C-section."

Kate put her hand over her mouth. "Oh no. I know Mia must be so upset."

"She is, but she understands. The doctor said the baby is just too big for her to safely give birth the old-fashioned way."

"So they are about to start?"

"Yeah, as soon as I get back in there. Just say a prayer for her."

"We will, man. Hang in there." Cooper said as Travis turned and walked back down the hallway.

"That's so scary."

Cooper stood behind her and put his arms around her.

"She's going to be okay. The baby is going to be great. C-sections are really quick, so there's going to be a baby very soon."

"Still, I'm going to say a prayer. It never hurts."

CHAPTER 10

KATE PACED BACK-AND-FORTH IN THE WAITING ROOM while Cooper napped in the corner. Wasn't it just like men to be able to sleep through something like this?

She thought about the tiny amount of time she'd gotten to spend with her sister so far, and she kept praying over and over again that everything was going fine in the operating room. She knew it was a C-section, and those were very commonplace, but this was her sister. Anything could go wrong with any surgery. She wouldn't rest until she heard everything was fine.

"Any word?" Kate turned to see her father standing in the doorway of the waiting room.

"Dad? I didn't think you were going to drive all the way here until the baby was born."

"I couldn't rest at home. Sylvia stayed behind with the dogs, and she's going to come once there's a baby."

"Jack?" Cooper said, rubbing his eyes as he woke up from his slumber.

"You're taking a nap while my daughter is over here pacing the floor?" he said jokingly.

"Sorry, that whole reality TV thing going on at the adventure center has worn me out."

"Yeah, Cooper and Travis think they're going to be TV stars," Kate said, laughing.

Cooper stood up and puffed out his chest. "You never know. I could be the next big thing."

"How is that going, anyway?" Jack asked.

"They are almost done shooting, so we will get our place back in a few days, thankfully. It was fun and interesting to watch, but the TV business isn't for me. It was great money, though."

"Hey y'all," Travis said from the doorway, a big smile on his face.

"Is everybody okay?" Kate asked, her hands in a prayer position under her chin.

"Mother and baby are fine."

"Well, is it a boy or a girl?" Cooper asked.

He grinned. "About fifteen minutes ago, Lacey Charlene was born."

A baby girl. Kate's heart welled up with gratitude. They both had daughters. Mia was going to get a lifelong best friend, just like Evie was to Kate. She felt so happy for her sister, and she couldn't wait to spoil her new niece rotten.

Mia laid in the bed holding her new baby daughter. Travis had gone to tell the family, and she had a few moments alone with her. All the medical professionals had left the room to give her some time.

The last few weeks, but certainly the last few hours, had been some of the most emotional of her life. Even losing her mother hadn't been as emotional as giving birth to her own daughter. The hormones were raging, and she didn't know which end was up.

She felt the void of her mother today. There was just nobody to replace her, even though she loved her husband and sister. She wanted her mother, and there was no way to have her. The feel of her mother hugging her right now was a longing that couldn't be filled.

"Hey, baby girl," she said to her new daughter. She was the most beautiful person in the world. A little button nose, bright blue eyes, porcelain white skin that would probably burn in the summertime just like Mia's did. She could see parts of herself and parts of Travis, like his wavy hair and his long fingers. Lacey was a perfect combination of the two of them. "I'm your momma. I am going to do everything I can to make life perfect for you, but if I screw up from time to time, you have to promise you'll still love me. But no matter what, no matter what you do, what mistakes you make, I will always love you."

She felt warm tears stinging her face as a wave of emotion she never felt before washed over her. It felt like she might never stop crying.

"Can I come in?" Mia looked up to see her sister standing in the doorway. All she could do was nod her head because she was crying too hard. Kate was crying too as she walked over to her bedside. "She is so beautiful!"

"I can't believe I have a daughter," Mia finally choked out. After feeling so alone when her mother died, her life was the fullest it had ever been. She knew her mother had a hand in that. A part of her imagined her mother in heaven holding Lacey's little hand and walking her to the gate, pointing her toward Mia's waiting arms.

"Lacey Charlene. It's a perfect name for a perfect little girl. Mom would be so proud."

"When they were doing the C-section, I could hear Momma talking to me. I know she was there."

"I'm so glad you're both okay."

"Do you want to hold her?"

Kate smiled. "Can I?"

"Of course. She needs to get to know her Aunt Kate."

Kate reached down and picked her up, cradling her in her arms. She stared down at her, looking into her bright blue eyes. She was so alert for a baby that had just been born. "I'm your Auntie Kate, and I'm going to spoil you rotten. If your mom and dad ever make you mad, you can always come to me. I'll always take your side."

Mia laughed as she watched her sister's first interaction with her daughter. She had so much happiness and gratitude in her heart that she feared it might burst. This was the happiest day of her life.

Kate put the finishing touches on the meatloaf and put it in the oven. It was the one request Mia had from the hospital before they came home. The doctor told her that her iron was a bit low, so her answer to that was to eat a big slab of beef. Kate didn't mind obliging her sister.

"Should I put the biscuits in the oven now?" Evie asked.

"Not yet. Those won't take so long. We'll wait until the meatloaf is almost done."

"I started packing my stuff last night. It won't be

long before I leave for basic training. I mean, I still have to take some tests, but I think I'll pass them."

"I don't think they let you take a lot with you, honey. Just the basics."

"You're probably right. So my stuffed animal collection will have to stay here?" she joked.

Kate laughed. "I do believe so."

"Are you nervous?" Cooper asked. He was mashing the potatoes, making sure to get out all the lumps. Kate always made sure she recruited him to help in the kitchen when she could.

"I'm a little nervous, but I think I'm more excited. I don't know what to expect."

"I think the physical challenges might be a difficult undertaking for you. I mean, you've never been super sporty," Kate said, chuckling. She recalled when Evie wanted to play softball in elementary school. She ended up picking weeds in the outfield and got bonked in the head by a softball. After a trip to the ER, Evie decided she wasn't into sports, after all.

"As long as I don't die while I'm trying to do the running part, I will consider that to be an impressive accomplishment."

"Is your dad coming today?" Cooper asked.

"Tomorrow. He wanted to give Travis and Mia some time to decompress before they came over. Of course, he's been sharing pictures all over social media of his new granddaughter. I think you've been replaced for a while, Evie."

Evie laughed. "That's okay. As soon as I start wearing my military uniform, he'll post pictures of me."

"So I guess it's going to be you and Lacey vying for attention for the rest of your lives."

Evie pulled the sweet tea out of the refrigerator. "I don't mind competing for his attention. That little baby won't win against me!" she joked, holding her fist in the air.

A few moments later, they could hear a car pulling up on the gravel driveway. Kate ran to the front window and saw Travis parking the car. He got out and walked around, opening the door for Mia.

She was wearing a sundress and carrying her new baby girl in her arms. Lacey was dressed in a little pink gown that Kate had brought to the hospital.

"Welcome home!" Kate yelled as she ran down the steps. Thankfully, the baby wasn't asleep because Kate was yelling so loudly that she would've definitely woken her up.

"Need help with something?" Cooper asked.

"No, I think we're good. All we have is the bag."

"Gosh, she's already looking older today," Kate said, looking down at her niece.

"Don't say that! I want her to stay this small forever."

"Good luck with that," Kate said, giggling.

Mia was still walking carefully, given that she had just had a C-section a couple of days before. Kate took her arm and helped her up the stairs while Travis stood on the other side.

When she got into the house, she sat on the sofa cradling her baby girl. Everybody sat around her, staring at the new member of their family.

"So, how's it feel to be a father?" Cooper asked.

"Amazing. I never knew I could love another human being so much," Travis said, staring down at his daughter as he sat beside Mia.

"I do think it's fair to warn both of y'all that once you've had a baby, nobody pays attention to you anymore. You are invisible adults because everyone wants to ogle the cute baby," Kate said, laughing.

"That's okay with us," Mia said, staring at Lacey.

Her sister looked so angelic and motherly. It was like a different person was sitting in front of her. She could feel the love in the room, and she knew Lacey was going to be adored for the rest of her life. Her parents were absolutely smitten with her.

"How are you feeling?"

Mia smiled. "Better than I thought I would be, actually. Maybe it's just the high of being a new mother, but I think I'm going to be okay."

"Still, she's going to take it easy going up and down those stairs. If I'm not here, can I count on you to help her, Kate?"

She nodded. "Of course."

"Do I smell meatloaf?"

Kate laughed. "That's quite a nose you have on you. It's in the oven, so you'll definitely get your beloved meatloaf today."

"Thanks for being there for us. It means a lot that you and Cooper sat in that waiting room for so long."

"You're my sister, and that's my niece. Of course we would wait. I'm just glad you made it through everything okay."

"We are, too. Honestly, I don't think I've ever felt so much happiness. I thought my heart might explode," she said, staring at her daughter.

Kate remembered those early days of motherhood when they placed Evie in her arms. She knew life would never be the same again. She couldn't stop staring at her new daughter.

"We're going to be here to help you raise that sweet little girl. I think we all value having family around."

"That's why Travis and I wanted to ask you and Cooper something."

"What?"

"Would you to do us the honor of being Lacey's

godparents?"

Kate put her hand over her heart and looked at Cooper, who appeared to be getting choked up himself.

"Of course!" Kate said, standing up and then leaning down to hug her sister.

"Cooper?"

He nodded and smiled, swallowing hard. "I would be honored."

Evie sat on her bed, thumbing through her scrapbooks. Since she was about ten years old, she had asked her mother for a scrapbook every year. She had stickers and all kinds of markers that she used to decorate them, but mostly they were full of memories. Pictures, movie ticket stubs, stuff from school.

It was hard for her to believe that she would leave home soon. She had depended on her mother for her entire life, and she was a little scared. As much as she wanted to be independent and start becoming an adult, she also wanted to slink back into being a child.

Sometimes, she had scary thoughts about what it would be like to be an adult out on her own. What if she didn't know how to do something? She didn't want to make big mistakes. At the same time, she knew that she would make mistakes, and she would have to call her mother for help.

"What are you doing?" Kate asked. She was standing in the doorway of Evie's room, looking around at all the boxes. Even though Evie couldn't take all of her stuff with her, she wanted to clear out the space as much as possible in case they needed the extra room for the B&B. Now that one room was a nursery, Evie's room might be needed.

"Just looking at some of my memories. Do you remember when I was in Girl Scouts?" she said, laughing as she pointed to a picture in her scrapbook. It was from when she won a baking contest where she was supposed to create her own recipe. In reality, she had cheated because her mother found the recipe online.

"I do. In fact, I still have some of your pins in my jewelry box. Those are some of my most prized possessions." Kate sat on the bed next to her.

"They are?"

"Of course. You earned those badges and pins. I'll never forget you walking over the little bridge so that I could pin them to your uniform."

"I don't remember that," she said, looking back down at her scrapbook. "Here's my first movie stub from when I went out with my friends alone. I remember when you let me go with my little friends, but you and the other mothers just sat in the back of the theater. We felt so big at twelve years old."

"It's hard to let our children go. We have to do it a little at a time, otherwise it breaks our hearts too much as mothers."

"Why are you packing up your room?"

"Because y'all might need it with one room being taken up for the nursery."

"Nobody expects you to give up your room, sweetie. Where will you stay when you come home to visit?"

"I'll just stay in whatever room is available at the time. It's no big deal."

"You'll always have a home here, no matter what."

"I'm a little nervous."

Kate rubbed her leg. "I know you are. That's natural."

"What if I can't do it? What if I'm not good enough to pass all the physical and mental challenges?"

"You try your hardest, and if it doesn't work out, we're always here to catch you. At your age, you're going to make mistakes. You're going to try some things that maybe don't work out. But that's fine because you have a support system."

"I just don't want to fail and disappoint everybody."

"Honey, you could never disappoint us. Just the

fact that you're going to serve your country is more than most people will ever be able to say in a lifetime. It's one of the hardest jobs in the world."

"Aside from motherhood?"

Kate laughed. "Let's just say they're neck and neck."

Evie looked back down at the scrapbook. "Here's that picture from when you and I went to the beach for the weekend. Remember that weird guy who tried to talk to us?"

"I do. But we did have that amazing cheesecake."

She nodded. "That was the best cheesecake I've ever had."

"I hope I've done right by you, Evie."

"What do you mean?"

"I hope I've prepared you for this world. I hope I have shown you love, grace, and strength. I hope by bringing you here, I've given you the gift of family. Mainly, I hope that when you look back, you're happy that I am your mother."

Evie's eyes watered. "I don't need to look back for that. I've always been glad you're my mother, even when I was acting like a brat." Kate smiled and put her arm around Evie, pulling her head to her shoulder.

"Kiddo, you'll always be my favorite."

~

Cooper had never been more nervous in his whole life. He was hoping the third time was a charm when he asked Kate to meet him on the square. The sun had just set, and people were still milling about a bit, going to dinner at the café or the Italian restaurant.

He hadn't given her much information other than he wanted to talk to her about something. Things had been so busy with the new baby and the business deal that he was afraid he would never get the chance to propose.

As he saw her walking down the sidewalk toward him, a smile on her face, his stomach felt like four million butterflies were zipping around. Actually, he had no idea what four million butterflies in his stomach would feel like, but he felt that was a fair representation of what he was feeling at the moment.

"Hey. What's all this?"

"Come in," he said, reaching his hand out and pulling her up the two steps into the gazebo. The town had lit it up with bunches of twinkle lights, and it was a magical place at night.

"Are you trying to woo me, Cooper? Because if so, you already wooed me a long time ago."

"I'm always trying to woo you," he said, smiling as he put his hands around her waist and pulled her closer, pressing a long kiss to her lips.

"Seriously, what's going on?" She looked around,

her eyes growing wide. "What are all these pictures doing here?"

Cooper had downloaded and printed twenty different pictures and had them all framed. They were scattered around the gazebo, sitting on folding tables he brought.

"These are some of our best memories. I thought you might want to see them." He walked her around, and she looked at them with her mouth hanging open.

"I can't believe you did all of this."

"I wanted to remind you of all the wonderful times we've had together so far."

She pointed to a photo. "This is right after we met. I think it was Mia's birthday party?"

"It was. And look at this one. This was when we took Evie to Atlanta to see that Broadway show at The Fox Theatre."

She smiled. "I'm so glad we got to do that. She loved it. And then we ate at that fancy restaurant where she tried escargot and spit it back onto her plate," Kate said, giggling.

"Here's one of my favorites from our special spot overlooking the mountains. It was a particularly beautiful day."

She picked up the photo and stared at it. "I remember that. The sky was the bluest I'd ever seen, and we watched the deer eating grass in the valley below us." She looked at him. "Is there some special occasion for all this?"

He stepped back, took a deep breath, and slowly blew it out. "Yes." Before he said anything else, a man playing guitar walked from out of the shadows and started playing their favorite song.

"Cooper, what's going on?" she asked, slowly.

The man smiled at her as he continued to play. Before he could lose his nerve, Cooper dropped onto one knee, pulling the blue box out of his pocket and holding it in the air, the twinkle lights making the diamond shimmer even more.

"Kate Miller, I have loved you since the moment I met you. I know you didn't love me at first, and that's okay. But I knew when I met you that there was no one else. I feel like I've known you my whole life, but more than that, I know I want to love you for the rest of my life."

She put her hands over her mouth, her eyebrows raised, obviously realizing what was happening. "Oh, my gosh…"

"Every day with you just makes me realize I am a better man than the day before because you're in my life. You are the air I breathe, you are the blue sky above the mountains, and you are the sunshine. I don't want to be on this planet without you. Tonight, we are surrounded by special memories from our past, but tomorrow I want to plan the memories we'll make in the future."

"I'm going to cry…"

"All of that to say, will you marry me?"

Before he could even get the words all the way out, Kate started jumping up and down, tears rolling down her cheeks.

"Yes! Of course!"

He stood up and put the ring on her finger, his hands shaking. She helped him slide it all the way on.

"I love you," he said, hugging her.

"I love you, too!"

"I've been trying to propose to you for weeks."

She tilted her head to the side. "Really? What happened?"

"We got interrupted. First by Deacon's, and then by a baby."

She laughed, more tears rolling out of her eyes. "I'm so sorry!"

Cooper put his hands on both sides of her face. "It doesn't matter anymore. I tried to find a perfect way to propose to you, and in the end, it didn't matter. I just needed to ask you."

"This is the most perfect way you could've ever asked me. I don't need my ring hidden in a dessert, or my name on a board at a baseball game. I love the way you proposed with our memories in this beautiful gazebo overlooking our beloved mountains. It's perfect for us."

"And you're perfect for me," he said, pressing his lips to hers.

EPILOGUE

ONE YEAR LATER

Kate stared into the full-length mirror. She had
never imagined herself wearing a wedding dress
again, but here she was. Of course, she had picked
something tasteful. The dress she wore wasn't like
what a twenty-something year old woman would
wear who was getting married for the first time. She
wasn't at that stage in life, and she was perfectly
happy with the dress she was wearing.

It was long, straight, and off-white with lace
accents. She wasn't wearing a veil but had her hair
pulled back in a ponytail with beautiful white
flowers around it.

"You just look gorgeous," Mia said, holding baby
Lacey on her hip. It was funny to see her holding
Lacey since Mia was so petite, and her daughter was

a big chunk. She had the fattest little legs Kate had ever seen, complete with rolls. She was worried Lacey was going to outgrow Mia before it was over with.

"Thank you. I can't believe I'm getting married today."

"We're almost ready. Is the bride ready?" Evie asked, poking her head into the room.

"Almost. How is my groom looking?"

"I'm not telling. I can't spoil the surprise."

Evie had come home on leave for the wedding, and Kate was so happy to have her there. Just the three women had been in her room all day, laughing, reminiscing, and getting ready for this new stage of life.

She and Cooper were going on an extended vacation to Italy, and she was so excited. She had never really traveled overseas, so this was going to be a whole new adventure. She was looking forward to real pasta and plenty of sightseeing with her new husband.

When her daughter left for basic training, Kate went through a sort of mourning period for a couple of weeks, but then she got on with it, like most women did when confronted with a challenge. She had kept moving forward, determined to make a life for herself and Cooper. Although she still missed her daughter when she wasn't there, she could feel peace about it now.

The business was thriving. Not only had Deacon's put her honey in over four-hundred stores, but now they were partnering with her on a brand new company that would make southern desserts. Her mother's recipes were going to be nationwide, and people would get to eat her pound cake, peach cobbler, and more.

Every time Kate saw Sweet Charlene's logo on anything, she was filled with a sense of pride. This mother that she had never met in person was forever etched in her heart. Even when mothers weren't there physically, they never left their children's hearts.

"Well, he had better be wearing that tuxedo we rented and not his blue jeans," Kate said, raising an eyebrow.

"Don't start getting mad at him before you even get married," Mia said, laughing.

She sat Lacey down on the floor with her toys. Lacey was already pulling up on furniture and had taken her first steps just a few days before. Of course, Mia and Travis had caught the whole thing on video because they took video of every moment of the day. Kate was convinced that there wasn't a second they weren't taking videos of their daughter.

"Are you ladies ready? The preacher is itching to start," Travis said, poking his head into the room.

"I'm ready," Kate said, smiling over at him. "Be down in a minute."

"You look beautiful, Kate," he said before shutting the door.

"Well, I guess this is it," Kate said, looking at her sister.

"I'm going to go on downstairs. I'll take Lacey with me," Evie said, obviously picking up on the fact that the sisters needed a moment together alone.

Mia walked over to her sister and took her hands. "I know you're nervous, but you and Cooper are meant for each other."

"I know we are. And I'm not nervous. I'm excited."

"Can you believe how far we've come?"

Kate smiled. "It's hard to believe that just a few years ago, I didn't even know I had a sister. And now look at us. Both married, you with a new baby and the B&B. Me with a thriving honey and dessert business. I have to think that our mother would be proud of us."

"I know she would be. I'll always be sad that you didn't get to know her here on earth, but she always knew you. And she's looking down on us right now."

"Can I have just a minute alone before I come downstairs?" Kate asked.

Mia nodded. "I'll see you down there."

Kate had chosen to get married at the B&B because she couldn't think of a better place. The whole backyard was set up for the wedding, and many people from town were there. She and Cooper would exchange vows in the gazebo he'd built after they'd first met. It seemed like the perfect place. Sweet Tea B&B was home, and she wanted so many more wonderful memories there.

As Mia left and shut the door behind her, Kate stood in the window and looked out over the beautiful Blue Ridge Mountains she had come to love so much.

She picked up the picture of her mother that sat on her nightstand and stared into the eyes that looked so much like hers. "Mom, I wish you could be here on my wedding day. Actually, I wish you could be here any day. I love you, even though I never got to hold your hand or smell your perfume. But you're here with me on my wedding day," she said, touching the necklace Mia had given her to wear. It was her mother's, and she had worn it almost every day when Mia was growing up. Kate put the picture down and turned toward the door.

As she walked down the stairs toward her wedding day, she stopped for a moment in the living room and looked around at the space that had given her so many good memories. She would forever be thankful for Sweet Tea B&B. After all, this place was her home. These people were her family, and she couldn't wait to continue building a legacy of love and family with them.

She walked to the French doors leading to the backyard and saw all the people waiting for her. The preacher. Her husband-to-be. Her daughter, sister, niece, and brother-in-law. Friends. Business associates.

This life she'd built from almost nothing was such a blessing to her. Everyone smiled as she opened the doors and stepped onto the patio leading to the stone walkway. At the end of it all was Cooper, smiling at her with a love so strong it felt like a magnet pulling her ever closer.

Her father stepped beside her and took her arm. "Are you ready, pumpkin?"

She smiled up at him. "I've never been more ready for something in my life."

"He's a good man."

She looked back at Cooper. "And he's mine."

They began the walk toward the gazebo, and Kate looked around at the small gathering of people. As an event planner, she'd planned some huge weddings before. Sometimes hundreds of people. But her wedding was perfect with a much smaller number of people. It wasn't the number of people that counted. To her, it was much more important that the people she loved had gathered to celebrate the love she and Cooper had built together.

It seemed like an eternity until she was standing at the altar in front of the preacher and Cooper.

"Hey," he whispered.

She smiled. "Hey."

"We're gathered together today to celebrate the union of a special couple, Kate and Cooper. Who gives this woman to this man today?"

Jack beamed. "I do." He took her hand and placed it in Cooper's, nodding at each of them before sitting beside Sylvia.

Cooper held her hand tightly and smiled at her. They turned to the preacher, who began speaking. Kate had no clue what he was saying because she was so focused on her soon-to-be husband looking at her.

She couldn't believe she was here. She was standing in the middle of her dream life, and she didn't even know it was a possibility a few short years ago. With the beautiful blue mountains in the background, she felt so much love and peace in her heart as she got ready to say "I do" to the man of her dreams.

"It's now time for the vows Kate and Cooper have written to express their love for one another. Kate?"

Her hands were shaking as she began to speak.

"Where do I begin? Cooper, the day we met, I thought you were the most annoying man I'd ever met." Everybody, including Cooper, laughed. "But then you started to grow on me, especially when you built this gazebo we're standing in right now. Who would've thought one day we'd stand here and promise to love each other forever? You are the best man I know. You're my rock, and you're my best friend. I promise to love you, support you, and always be your biggest fan."

His eyes welled with tears. He swallowed hard and began his vows. "Kate, I loved you from the moment I met you, even though you thought I was annoying. I probably was because you're always right."

"Smart man!" Jack yelled from the audience, causing everyone to laugh again.

Cooper smiled at Jack and continued. "You're the most beautiful woman I've ever seen. Your smile still makes me melt, and your strength inspires me everyday. I will love you until there are no more breaths to take. All of my dreams include you, and I can't wait for us to go on adventures together as husband and wife. I will always be there for you, and I will always protect you. There is no love that compares to ours, and I will fiercely guard that forever. I love you."

"I love you," she mouthed through tears.

The rest of the service was a blur as they lit the unity candle and listened to a local person sing their favorite love song.

"Cooper, you may kiss your bride!" the preacher finally yelled. He put his hand behind her neck and dipped her backward, pressing a long kiss to her lips. Everything was in slow motion as Kate felt the wave of his love overwhelm her.

As they walked down the aisle back toward Sweet Tea B&B, her heart swelled. This had to be heaven because she couldn't imagine anything better. Life could really change on a dime.

***

To read more Rachel Hanna books, visit www. RachelHannaAuthor.com.

Made in United States
Orlando, FL
22 November 2022

24881705R00107